About this Book

This book contains three mystery stories with a difference. The difference is that you have to solve the mystery yourself.

Each mystery story contains a series of puzzles which must be solved for the next part of the story to make sense. Find the solution to all the puzzles and you will solve the mystery.

Clues and evidence are lurking in the pictures and the words, so keep your eyes open and think carefully. Some of the puzzles relate to previous pages, so you will need to flick back to hunt for clues.

If you get stuck, there are extra clues to help you. These are printed in a special, cryptic way, so you will have to work out how to read them first. If you have to admit defeat, you will find all the answers, with detailed explanations, at the end of each story.

D1642689

ESCAPE FROM BLOOD CASTLE

Contents

About this Story

Escape from Blood Castle is a strange and exciting adventure. Its hero is Intrepid Ivor. Follow him through the underground maze, on to the roof and down into the dungeons of Blood Castle as he hunts for the all-important Papers.

The story begins over the page. Just start reading. At the bottom of the page, there is a puzzle to solve. Don't turn over until you have found the answer. If you get stuck, there are extra clues on page 41. You will find all the answers on pages 42 to 48.

COUSIN BORIS

INTREPID IVOR

THE FRIENDLY SPIDER

THE MOUSE WHO HELPS IVOR

3

Intrepid Ivor and the Evil Baron

Ivor's heart thumped as he crouched, shivering, among the bushes. Looming in front of him was the object of his thoughts for many months – Blood Castle, home of the man Ivor knew as Cousin Boris, but who now refused to answer to anything but The Baron. Perhaps he should just turn round now and run home.

Ivor thought of his favourite TV heroes and pulled himself together. He couldn't let himself be cheated of wealth and title by his creepy cousin. His friends would never call him Intrepid Ivor again if he funked this.

Pausing only to check he still had his trusty survival kit in his pockets (useful things, such as chewing gum, pepper, nylon thread and half a chocolate bar), Intrepid Ivor made his way towards the castle's west wall, darting stealthily from bush to bush.

How to get in was the first problem. Ivor thoughtfully sucked his finger where it had caught on the sharp hook in his pocket and surveyed the scene in front of him. Suddenly he worked out what to do . . .

DON'T TURN THE PAGE YET.

This picture shows the building as Ivor saw it. How and where did Ivor get in?

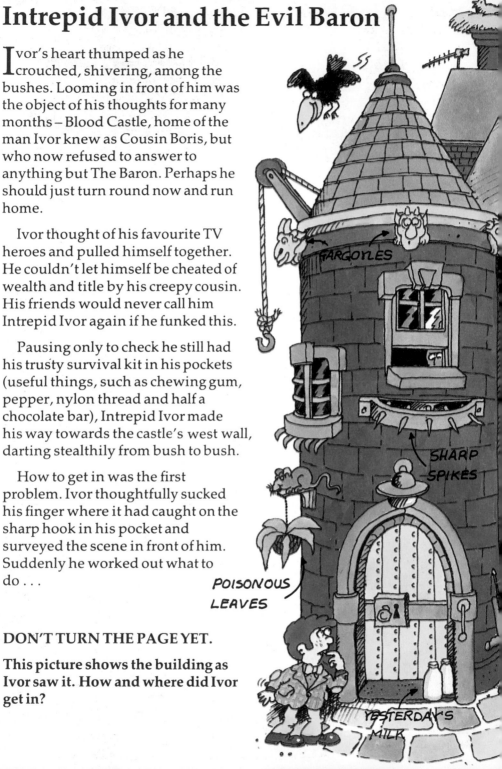

GARGOYLES

SHARP SPIKES

POISONOUS LEAVES

YESTERDAY'S MILK

4

Inside Blood Castle

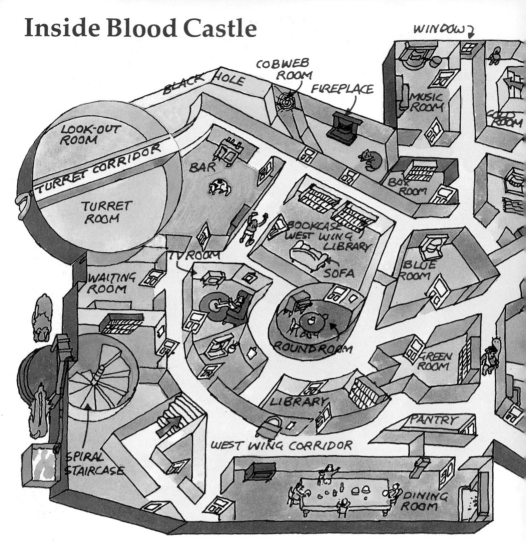

It was pitch black inside. Ivor shuffled along, feeling his way along the wall with his hand. He could see nothing – it was like walking blindfold. His ears strained for the slightest sound, but there was none.

He felt the corridor curve to the left and then turn sharp right. For a short distance the surface beneath his fingers became very smooth, but soon changed again to the same roughish texture as before. A dozen or so steps further on he felt the same temporary smoothness beneath his fingertips again. For the first time he could hear something. He paused. A faint snoring sort of sound reached his ears. He crept onwards – a slight left turn, followed by quite a sharp one and then a shaft of light.

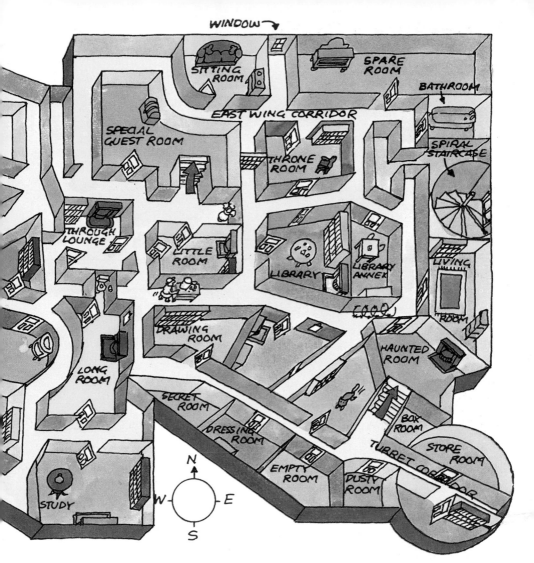

At last he could have a look at the map in his pocket and try to work out where he was.

Ivor's intention was to find the vital Papers which would show who was the rightful heir to Blood Castle. He had been told that they were in a room with two doors on adjacent walls and a fireplace on the wall

opposite the larger door, with a large bookcase to its left.

DON'T TURN THE PAGE YET.

Above is a copy of the map Ivor carried in his pocket.
    Where is Ivor now?
    Which room should he go to and which route should he take to get there?

The Locked Door

BORIS

WASTE PAPER BASKET

AUNT MATILDA'S SPARE SPECTACLES

PEAR PIE

8

BELL PULL

MATILDA

UNCLE SPIKE'S WALKING STICKS

COAL BUCKET

FELIX

COLD TEA

With shaking hand, Ivor edged the door open. Yes, there was the fireplace facing him with a bookcase to its left. It must be the right room. He opened the door a little wider and crept in.

A few steps took him to the middle of the room. Then his heart stopped as he heard a loud bang behind him, followed by the unmistakable sound of a key turning slowly in a rusty lock. He rushed to the door in a panic. It was indeed locked. The other door! Of course that was locked too.

As he frantically searched the room for a way out, Ivor almost forgot why he was there in the first place. The Papers! He might as well use his energy looking for them.

Nothing. In despair, Ivor sank down next to the bookcase and stared at the books.

''You've made a mess of this, Ivor,'' he thought to himself.

Suddenly he realized there was something very odd about the books. Picking a scrap of paper out of the waste-paper basket, he started scribbling furiously.

''Got it!'' he said aloud and jumped to his feet. In a few seconds he was out of the room.

DON'T TURN THE PAGE YET.

What did Ivor see and how did he get out of the room?

9

Another Map?

I vor found himself in another room. He tried the door straight away. Whew! It wasn't locked.

He leaned against it, breathing a sigh of relief and realized, as he did so, that he still had in his hand the screwed-up scrap of paper he had been scribbling on. He was about to toss it away when he saw it had something on the back. He smoothed it out on the table and found that it was a map. It looked just like the one he had in his pocket. But was it really the same?

It took a minute or two for Ivor to check his heavily laden pockets, but eventually he found his own map, neatly folded up.

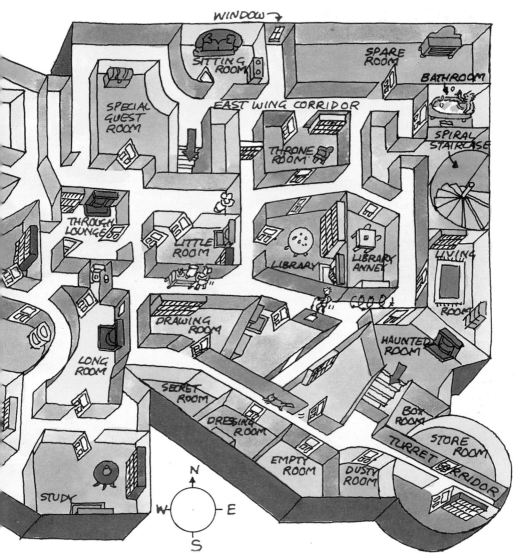

He compared the two maps very carefully. There were lots of tiny differences. Suddenly Ivor knew why he hadn't found the Papers – he'd been in the wrong room all the time. What's more, he knew what he had to do next.

Quickly snatching a useful-looking box from the table, he set off.

DON'T TURN THE PAGE.

This is the map Ivor found. Compare it with the one he had in his pocket (on pages 6-7) and see if you can find all the differences. How did Ivor know he'd been in the wrong room?

Where did he set off to?

Ivor Meets the Tea Trolley

Feeling rather pleased with himself, Ivor quickly made his way to the stairs.

The noise was a shock. In his haste, he had forgotten that danger could be lurking round every corner. He thought it sounded a bit like crockery rattling, but decided he was being silly. It was obviously something much more sinister. It was getting louder too.

Suddenly all was quiet again. A friendly looking spider scuttled across the floor in front of him. Ivor enticed it into the little box he had in his hand. It made him feel better to have a friend – even if it was only a spider.

After waiting for what seemed like ages, Ivor spread himself round the corner at the top of the stairs. He was in an empty room. As he tip-toed out of the door and into the corridor, he could smell something which reminded him of strong, well-brewed tea.

Ivor crept along the corridors until eventually he spotted the source of the smell. There, all alone, was a tea trolley. A huge urn steamed gently among piles of the most delicious looking cakes and buns.

ARTHUR

PEARL'S FAVOURITE DRINK

FEL

SPIDER HOLE

GRANDFATHER BLOOD'S ARABIAN VASE

Ivor couldn't resist cakes and there didn't seem to be anyone about . . .
DON'T TURN THE PAGE YET.

Ivor strained his eyes and just managed to read the notice propped up on the tea trolley. We've magnified it so you can read it. Which cakes can Ivor eat safely?

The Family

Ivor picked the stickiest looking cake and bit into it. The red jam ran down his chin. "Yum yum, terrif...", he thought, then something seemed to go wrong with his brain. The Tea lady's hideously ugly face loomed very close to his own. The ground seemed closer than it should be too...

The bumping, banging and rattling was making his head ache and he felt sick, but luckily the brain disease seemed to have gone away. He cautiously moved his body and found he was sitting on the tea trolley. His feet and hands were roped to the four corners of it.

A strangled grunt and a violent jolt of the trolley prompted Ivor to peer cautiously out, but all he could see

was a frightened spider, the twin of his friend in the box, scurrying down the corridor.

He stared again at the Tea Lady. Could she be one of Boris's "family" in disguise? He thought about some photographs he had once seen of them.

A sudden awful stomach-lurch told him they were in a lift – going down. "That's the one!" thought Ivor, just as his stomach settled in its right place again and the lift doors opened. "That might be useful", he thought and dozed off again.

DON'T TURN THE PAGE YET.

Here are the photographs of the family which Ivor had seen. Which of them do you think is the tea lady?

Captured!

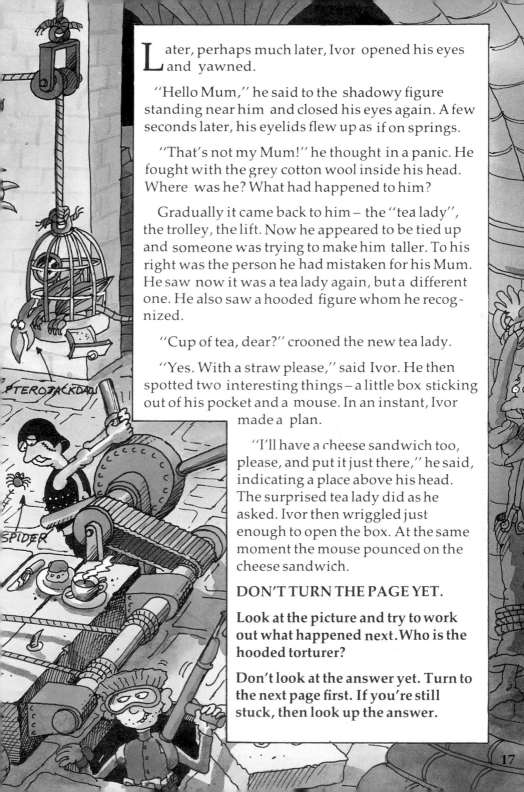

Later, perhaps much later, Ivor opened his eyes and yawned.

"Hello Mum," he said to the shadowy figure standing near him and closed his eyes again. A few seconds later, his eyelids flew up as if on springs.

"That's not my Mum!" he thought in a panic. He fought with the grey cotton wool inside his head. Where was he? What had happened to him?

Gradually it came back to him – the "tea lady", the trolley, the lift. Now he appeared to be tied up and someone was trying to make him taller. To his right was the person he had mistaken for his Mum. He saw now it was a tea lady again, but a different one. He also saw a hooded figure whom he recognized.

"Cup of tea, dear?" crooned the new tea lady.

"Yes. With a straw please," said Ivor. He then spotted two interesting things – a little box sticking out of his pocket and a mouse. In an instant, Ivor made a plan.

"I'll have a cheese sandwich too, please, and put it just there," he said, indicating a place above his head. The surprised tea lady did as he asked. Ivor then wriggled just enough to open the box. At the same moment the mouse pounced on the cheese sandwich.

DON'T TURN THE PAGE YET.

Look at the picture and try to work out what happened next. Who is the hooded torturer?

Don't look at the answer yet. Turn to the next page first. If you're still stuck, then look up the answer.

PTEROJACKDAW

SPIDER

What Really Happened?

These pictures show what happened in the dungeon during the chaos that followed the spider's escape – or do they?

Some of these things happened, but not in the order shown. Can you sort out which pictures tell the truth and in what order?

The lever pulls the trapdoor open, letting the balls through.

The mouse jumps on Roxanne's nose and she runs away.

The mouse jumps on to the sandwich, pushing the lever down.

The pterojackdaw's cage falls on Horace's head and knocks him out.

The pterojackdaw gets free and attacks Arthur.

The noose tightens round Roxanne's foot, tripping her up and knocking over the tea trolley.

The rope holding the pendulum burns and it crashes down.

18

Ivor wriggles up the bed and is able to unhook his handropes.

Arthur is submerged by the contents of the tea trolley.

The spider frightens Horace who lets go of the wheel, loosening Ivor's ropes.

The chandelier is winched up by the machine and the candles burn through the rope holding the cage.

Ivor adds to his "useful" things

The dungeon floor was littered with bits and pieces. Ivor couldn't resist cramming some of them into his already overloaded pockets. Here you can see what he picked up.

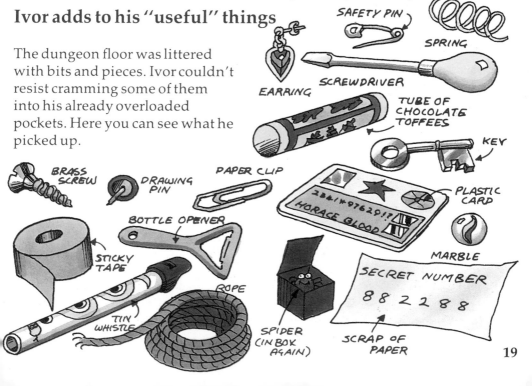

19

Escape from the Dungeon

ROXANNE'S MUMMY

USED TO CONTAIN A PLANT

GRANDFATHER BLOOD'S BICYCLE

FRUIT MACHINE

HORACE'S DISGUISE

PEARL'S BICYCLE

SPIDER-EATING PLANT

THE MOUSE THAT HELPED IVOR ESCAPE

SLIME

Ivor grabbed a sandwich from the overturned tea trolley and, with pockets and cheeks bulging, he thought about what to do next.

Obviously he must get out of the dungeon before Horace and the others came to. Then he must find the lift and the Papers. But which of the seven identical green doors should he go through?

He had been half-asleep, half-awake while the tea trolley had trundled him along. Hazy memories floated into his mind. Yes, he

AWFUL ARTHUR'S PRIZE PIRANHA

HORACE'S FRIENDS

BLOOD FAMILY COAT OF ARMS

5

6

7

POISONOUS PALM

ARTHUR'S BICYCLE

NORMAN'S BICYCLE

FRUIT MACHINE

STINGING FERN

FRUIT MACHINE

MORE OF PEARL'S EMPTIES

PEARL'S EMPTIES

TO THE SEWER

UNCLE SPIKE'S LOST ROLLER SKATE

remembered entering the dungeon now. He had passed close to a fruit machine. It was on his left . . . or was it right? He remembered the trolley's back right-hand wheel brushing past a bicycle and almost knocking it over, too. He concentrated harder and remembered something odd

hanging from the ceiling and some crates in front of the fruit machine.

DON'T TURN THE PAGE YET.

Which of the doors in the picture should Ivor go through?

Norman and the Pinball Machine

Having made his decision, Ivor pushed the door. It wouldn't open. He pushed again, leaning his whole weight on it, and suddenly it swung open. He stumbled through into the gloom and found himself face to chest with nephew Norman.

"Hello," said Norman. "Who are you? Come and play pinball with me."

Ivor gulped and produced what he hoped was a friendly smile. He'd never come higher than 153rd on the school pinball ladder. Norman's vice-like grip on his arm didn't encourage him to refuse and he found himself being led along the corridor.

After two left and three right turns, Norman opened a door.

"Wow!" said Ivor. The most amazing pinball machine Ivor had ever seen stood in the middle of the room. It was huge and covered with brightly coloured pictures and lights.

"My turn first," said Norman, who immediately sent the first ball whizzing round the machine. Ivor's eyes grew bigger and rounder as he watched. This boy was GOOD. He notched up a score of 208,361 with one ball!

"OK", said Norman, "now you've got to match my score exactly, or I shan't let you leave the room."

DON'T TURN THE PAGE YET.

What route should Ivor's ball take round the machine to match Norman's score?

TOP SCORER: G. BLOOD

208,361

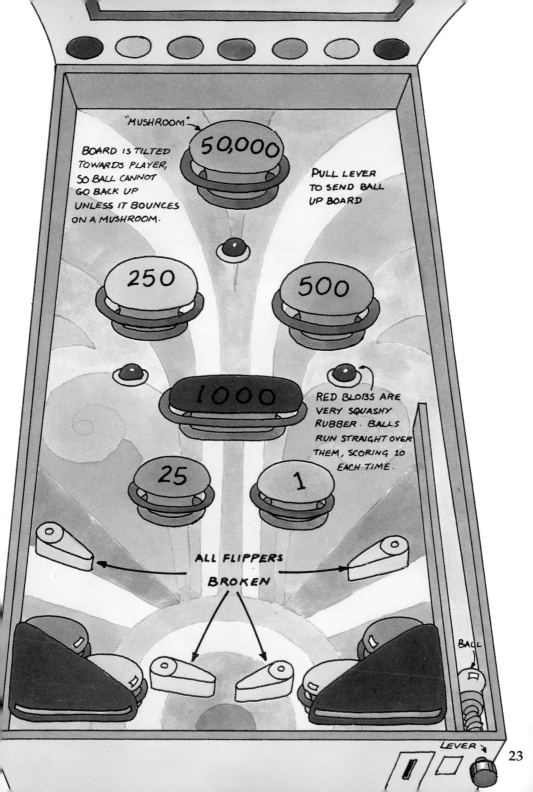

"MUSHROOM"

50,000

BOARD IS TILTED TOWARDS PLAYER, SO BALL CANNOT GO BACK UP UNLESS IT BOUNCES ON A MUSHROOM.

PULL LEVER TO SEND BALL UP BOARD

250

500

1000

RED BLOBS ARE VERY SQUASHY RUBBER. BALLS RUN STRAIGHT OVER THEM, SCORING 10 EACH TIME.

25

1

ALL FLIPPERS

BROKEN

BALL

LEVER

23

The Surprising Toffees

Norman jumped up and down hysterically. "3325! You'll have to stay here for ever!"

Ivor's heart couldn't sink any further. He reached into his pocket and pulled out the tube of chocolate toffees he'd found in the torture room.

"Want one?" he said, and Norman's greedy eyes lit up. He took ten and crammed them all in his mouth at once. Disgusted, Ivor took one for himself and was on the point of putting it in his mouth, when he noticed Norman's face change. He made a strangled sound and crashed heavily to the floor.

Horrified, Ivor dropped the toffee he was holding and let the rest of the packet fall after it.

He turned to go but the walls were completely covered with shelves. There was no sign of the door. He scanned the room, searching for a clue to the way out. The cursor on the computer screen winked at him.

"Which way?" it asked. Ivor felt like kicking it. He pressed some keys and got a picture on the screen.

"Oh, I see," he said.

DON'T TURN THE PAGE YET.

What did Ivor do next?

CHOCOLATE TOFFEES

Blood Castle Underground

Ivor squeezed through the hole and found himself in a twisty passage. Somehow or other he must find his way to the lift and get back upstairs. **DON'T TURN THE PAGE YET.**

Work out where Ivor is and which route he should take to the lift.

(NOTE: SOME OF THE PASSAGES GO BEHIND OTHERS — YOU ARE ALLOWED TO GO ALONG THESE.)

PORTRAITS OF BORIS CONCEAL TV CAMERAS — AVOID THEM.

AWFUL ARTHUR'S PRACTICE TANK

SHARK

BORIS →

NEPHEW NORMAN

BORIS

TRAP DOOR

TRAP-DOOR IN FLOOR

PAULINE

PEARL'S HIDEAWAY

SLIPPERY SHAFT

SHARP SPIKES

ROXANNE'S MAKE-UP ROOM

SNAKE PIT

WAY OUT

BORIS →

26

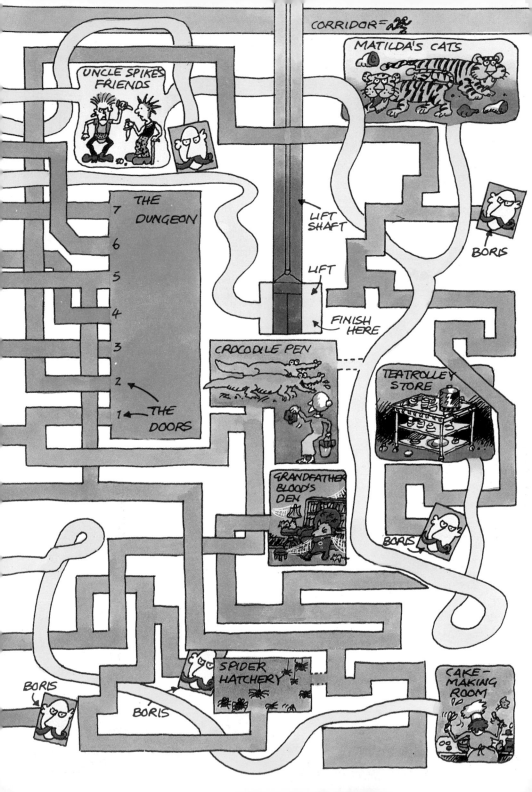

Ivor Goes Up

At last Ivor found himself standing in front of a lift. He stepped inside and the door closed behind him. The control panel looked like an aeroplane flight deck and was so high up Ivor had to stand on tip-toe to see it. There were flashing coloured lights, digital displays, dials and gauges, and a set of buttons numbered from zero to nine. Ivor did some calculations and decided which button to press.

Nothing happened. On closer examination, he realized that the buttons were shielded by a layer of clear perspex.

?

Ivor stared thoughtfully at the panel. He then started poking at it with something he found in his pocket. Ah! Something was happening. The perspex panel slid across to expose the buttons, so Ivor pressed some of them and, at last, the lift set off upwards.

A voice in his ear made Ivor jump higher than the control panel. It seemed to be coming from the portrait of Boris hanging on the wall.

"He's escaped. Guard the East Turret immediately. Repeat. Guard the East Turret."

"Gosh," thought Ivor, "They must think I'm Horace!"

The lift stopped as suddenly as it had started, the doors slid open and Ivor stepped out.

DON'T TURN THE PAGE YET.

How did Ivor make the lift work and why did "they" think he was Horace?

SPIKE

On the Roof

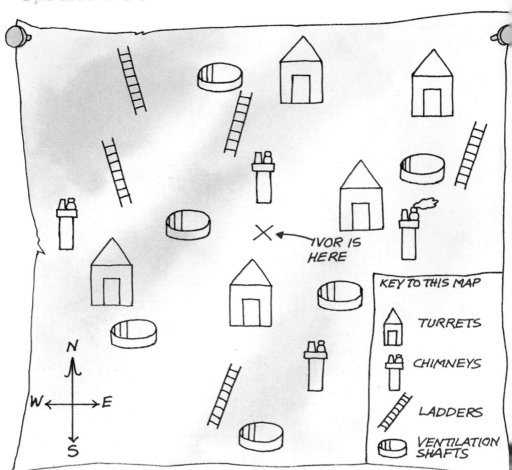

KEY TO THIS MAP

TURRETS

CHIMNEYS

LADDERS

VENTILATION SHAFTS

IVOR IS HERE

N
W ← → E
S

A cold wind hit Ivor in the face. He was outdoors! He walked to the nearest wall, leaned over and pulled sharply back. He was an awfully long way from the ground.

Ivor threaded his way through the ventilation shafts and chimneys. He was wondering where to go next when he came across a map.

"If they are so keen on guarding the east turret," he thought, "there must be something of interest there. It must be that one . . . or that one. Hmmm, which direction is east?"

DON'T TURN THE PAGE YET.

Above you can see the map Ivor is looking at and, on the right, the roofscape views (not in order) he sees by turning through 90° at a time. What is the colour of the door on the east turret?

31

What the Papers Say

Ivor kicked open the brightly painted door like people do in gangster films and waited to see what would happen.

"Stick 'em up!" screamed a harsh voice and Ivor did so, terrified.

"Stick 'em up! Steeck 'emm uppp! Steeeeeck 'emmmmmmmmmm uppppppppppppppppp! Whirr clank."

Ivor pushed the door again. Silence. There was no-one in sight. He went in, almost tripping over an ancient tape recorder and the deep carpet. Expensive-looking paintings hung on the walls. There was certainly something of interest here. He glanced through an open door and saw a sumptuously furnished office, complete with antique desk.

The room was empty, so Ivor tip-

TESTAMENT

OKER TABLE, MY
VER SAFETY PINS
SON SPIKE, MY
MY DIVING
ON TO ART

ANTIQUE SIL
BOXES TO M
EG TO HERBER
HARPOON COLLECT
NHA BIRD AND MY
TO BABY NORMAN
F 'THE CROCODILE' AN
TO MATILDA AN
STRET

THIS IS
OF GRA
I HEREB
COLLECTION
AND MY JUKE
WOODEN
GEAR AND
MY PIRAN
MACHINE
COPIES
MONTHL
ENT

toed in. Perhaps the Papers would be here – they would surely have been moved from their original hiding place by now. He searched the desk drawers but found nothing. He glanced around the room but all he could see was a very dirty, dog-eared envelope which had fallen on the floor. He picked it up and looked inside. All it contained was torn scraps of paper. He tipped them out on to the desk, idly wondering what they could be.

Then a few words caught his eye: "Last will . . . Blood . . . wealth . . . ." and he frantically started putting together this paper jigsaw puzzle.

DON'T TURN THE PAGE YET.

What do the scraps of paper say?

33

Ivor Meets Boris

Ivor's brain hurt . . . and his heart too. This wasn't what he'd expected to find! He stuffed the scraps back into the envelope, pushed it into his pocket and turned to leave the room.

There, outlined in the doorway, was Boris.

Ivor wasn't even scared any more. He was too disheartened to care what happened next. He stared coolly at the tall, still figure.

What did happen next surprised him. He heard his own voice cry out.

"You're not Boris!" it said.

DON'T TURN THE PAGE YET.

How did Ivor know that the man in front of him was not Boris?

BORIS: A STUDY OF HANDS

MY EAR BY ARTHUR

ROXANNE

THE DESK

THE TWINS AT PLAY

35

The Prisoner

Ivor darted for the door and slipped past Boris's legs before Boris had time to close his mouth. Down the corridor, up some steps and through a door sped Ivor. He waited breathing heavily. There was no sign that he had been followed.

The room was very gloomy.

BORIS BY MATILDA

He could hardly see anything at all, but he could hear some faint sounds coming from somewhere to his left. He found a door. The noises were definitely coming from the other side of it.

The door was stiff and creaky but there was more light on the other side. Ivor couldn't believe his eyes. There, inside a gigantic cage, was Boris! A few seconds' thought led Ivor to the conclusion that it must be the real Boris, his genuine cousin.

"Ivor! How pleased I am to see you!" said Boris.

Ivor didn't reply. He was still suspicious of Boris, real or not.

"I've been a prisoner here since Grandfather Blood died and Wicked Wilf came back from Australia and started impersonating me. You've got to help me to escape."

"OK," Ivor said, after a while. "I've got an idea. Hand me that rope."

Ivor then proceeded to free Boris from his cage.

DON'T TURN THE PAGE YET.

What did Ivor do to release Boris from the cage?

The Escape Plan

A scrap of paper on the floor caught Ivor's eye. He picked it up. This is it:

GRANDSON IVOR, PROVIDING MY DAUGHTER MATILDA IS STILL ALIVE AND MY

"What's that?" asked Boris. Ivor showed him and the rest of the pieces he'd found in the envelope.

"The Will! We've no time to lose! We must find Aunt Matilda and get out of Blood Castle as soon as possible, so we can claim our inheritances. I bet I can guess where she'll be and, what's more, I know how we can escape!"

"How?" said Ivor, disbelievingly.

"Easy! Grandfather Blood gave me this just before he died. Thank goodness I can read music! You must have seen Aunt Matilda somewhere in the castle. Think carefully."

DON'T TURN THE PAGE YET.

This is what Grandfather Blood gave Boris. How can they use it to help them escape? (You don't have to be able to read music to work it out.) Where did they find Aunt Matilda?

The Truth at Last

Boris's plan worked like a charm. Aunt Matilda was where Ivor had seen her earlier and the three of them made their escape, using Grandfather Blood's music and Ivor's tin whistle.

As they stood outside breathing the fresh air, Ivor realized they were not a stone's throw from where he had started, goodness knows how long ago. Quickly and quietly they made their way through the gate and up the tree-lined road beyond it. When they reached the top of the hill, they paused to look back. They saw the dim shapes of "Boris", Herbert and Horace loading suitcases into Grandfather Blood's battered old Rolls Royce.

"They're running away!" cried Ivor.

"Let them", said Boris. "They won't get far."

They watched while the ancient Rolls chugged through the gate and out of sight. An hour later, tired and breathless, they reached the home of Mr Sprog, the Blood family's lawyer.

Mrs Sprog produced a wonderful tea for them, which they attacked gratefully while they told Mr Sprog their story. After a while, Ivor looked at Boris thoughtfully and said, "I don't understand how you came to have the scrap of the Will which mentioned me."

Boris explained that Wicked Wilf had torn this piece off himself and that he, Boris, had managed to hide it and keep it safe.

"But", said Boris, "What I don't understand is what would have happened to the legacy if Aunt Matilda were not still alive?"

They all looked at Aunt Matilda, who had turned slightly pink.

"Oh well", she said, and produced a scrap of paper from her handbag. This is what it said:

" . . . otherwise everything is to go to World Spider Sanctuary."

She explained her worry that Pearl's passion for spiders might make her do something dangerous.

"Well, there's only one question left," said Mr Sprog. "Who tore up the Will?"

They all looked blankly at each other.

Do you know?

Clues

Page 4

Ivor enters in the normal way. He needs something first though. Search the picture carefully for the key to the problem and then work out how he gets hold of it. Beware the SNAKE PIT.

Page 6

Start at the door in the turret in the top left hand corner of the map. Ivor feels his way with his left hand. Smooth areas are doors.

Page 8

Ivor saw the titles were in code. He decoded the title of a large book and found it to be "Snake Charming for Beginners." Try decoding the others.

Page 10

There are at least 23 differences. The most important ones concern the stairs.

Page 12

Read the list carefully to work out what each bit means. There are 15 safe cakes.

Page 14

The "tea lady" need not be female. Look for tell tale strands under the wig.

Page 16

The "tea lady" did a quick change. The mouse is quite heavy. What does the lever do?

Page 18

There are 3 false pictures. The rest are true.

Page 20

This one's easy – you don't need a clue!

Page 22

Start by bouncing the ball from 50000 to 500 and back three times.

Page 24

The picture on the screen corresponds to the floor of the room. Ivor thought the second largest rectangle might be the rug.

Page 26

The maze is quite easy. But if you take a wrong route, don't worry. You might see something that comes in useful later on.

Page 28

Look at the things Ivor picked up in the torture room (see page 19). He used two of these.

Page 30

The smoke gives it away.

Page 32

You could trace or photocopy these pieces, cut them out and stick them together to read them.

Page 34

There are portraits of Boris all through the book. Compare them with the figure in the doorway.

Page 36

Notice the pulley in the ceiling, the greasy ring in the top of the cage, the hook on the rope and the ladder.

Page 38

Look on pages 26-27 for Aunt Matilda and a way out. To escape they need one of the things Ivor found on page 19 and Grandfather Blood's Little tune. One of the books on page 8 might be useful too.

Page 40

Look at the portraits throughout the book. They're not all of Boris. Maybe they're not all portraits either.

41

Answers

Pages 4-5

Ivor notices a key on the window ledge. He climbs up by the route shown and sits on the ledge above the window. He uses the nylon thread and sharp hook from his pocket to make a fishing line and "fishes" for the key. He then climbs down by the same route, unlocks the front door and goes in.

(Did you think you could go in through the open door? This isn't a good idea – the backwards writing on this door says "SNAKE PIT".)

Ivor sits here to fish for key.

Key

Ivor climbs up this way

Pages 6-7

Here you can see the route Ivor takes and the room he goes to.

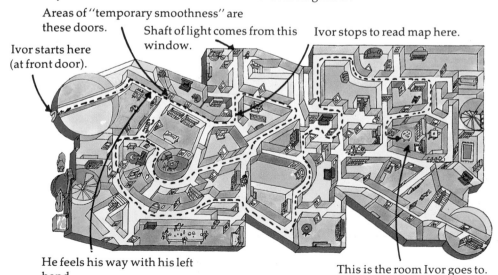

Areas of "temporary smoothness" are these doors.

Shaft of light comes from this window.

Ivor stops to read map here.

Ivor starts here (at front door).

He feels his way with his left hand.

This is the room Ivor goes to.

42

Pages 8-9

The book titles are all written backwards. The second book from the right on the bottom shelf reads "HANDLE PULL HERE". He pulls it and the bookcase opens revealing the room beyond. (Try decoding the other titles – they may give you some ideas about things that happen later.)

Pages 10-11

Ivor spots that the arrows on the stairs go in different directions and that the new map shows more of the west outside wall. He concludes that his map shows the wrong floor and he needs to search the equivalent room upstairs. He makes for the nearest stairs following the route shown*. Did you find all the other differences too? They are ringed here.

Ivor starts in this room (downstairs).

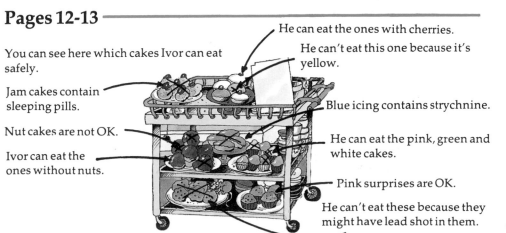

*Ivor is, of course, still on the ground floor. We have shown the route here on the first floor map, but the route on the ground floor is exactly the same.

He takes this route.

He comes up these stairs.

Pages 12-13

You can see here which cakes Ivor can eat safely.

Jam cakes contain sleeping pills.

Nut cakes are not OK.

Ivor can eat the ones without nuts.

He can eat the ones with cherries.

He can't eat this one because it's yellow.

Blue icing contains strychnine.

He can eat the pink, green and white cakes.

Pink surprises are OK.

He can't eat these because they might have lead shot in them.

The "tea lady" is Horace. The strands of red hair give him away. The Pearl "look-alike" wig hides his scar.

Here you can see what happens in the dungeon. The hooded torturer is Horace. His scar is the clue.

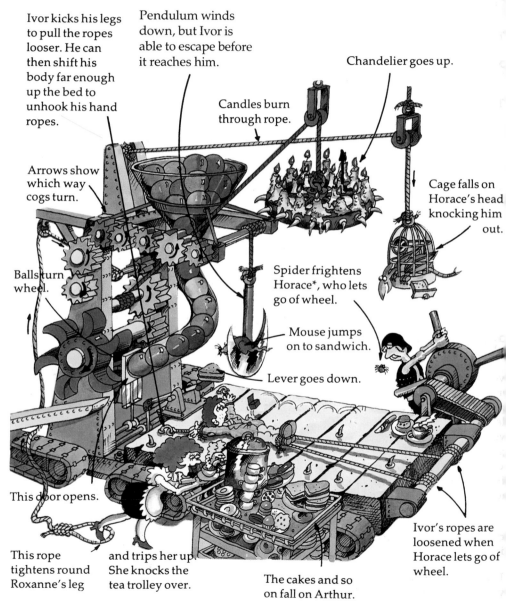

Ivor kicks his legs to pull the ropes looser. He can then shift his body far enough up the bed to unhook his hand ropes.

Pendulum winds down, but Ivor is able to escape before it reaches him.

Chandelier goes up.

Candles burn through rope.

Arrows show which way cogs turn.

Cage falls on Horace's head knocking him out.

Balls turn wheel.

Spider frightens Horace*, who lets go of wheel.

Mouse jumps on to sandwich.

Lever goes down.

This door opens.

Ivor's ropes are loosened when Horace lets go of wheel.

This rope tightens round Roxanne's leg and trips her up. She knocks the tea trolley over.

The cakes and so on fall on Arthur.

*You know Horace is frightened of spiders from page 15.

he pictures go in this order: 3, 10, 1, 6, 11, 4, 9, 8.
ictures 2, 5 and 7 did not happen. The pendulum comes
own (follow the cogs round to see why) but Ivor has
lready escaped.

he only door which fits the description completely is door 5.

his is the route Norman's ball took.

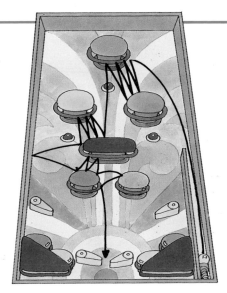

vor spots that Nephew Norman has a book
n computer games. When he sees the
uestion "WHICH WAY" on the screen, he
ecides to try typing in directions, as you
ould if playing a computer adventure
ame. When he types "DOWN", a diagram
omes up on the screen. Ivor realizes that
his corresponds to a floor plan of the room
e is in.

Ivor then lifts the rug and finds the
rapdoor, which he opens by pulling the
ing.

Perhaps you can work out the route
vor's ball took on the pinball machine.)

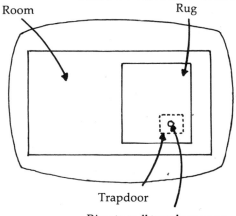

Room

Rug

Trapdoor

Ring to pull trapdoor open.

Pages 26-27

—— Ivor's route from the dungeon to Norman's room.

---- Ivor follows this route from Norman's room to the lift.

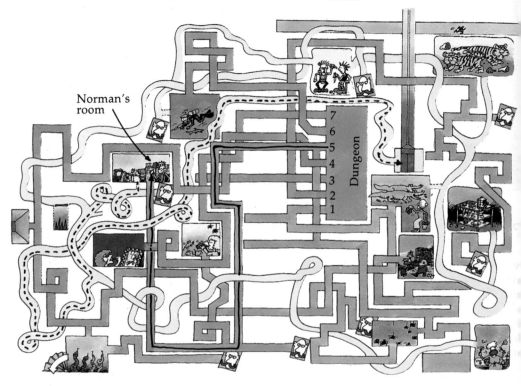

Norman's room

Dungeon

7
6
5
4
3
2
1

Pages 28-29

Ivor puts the "credit card" he found in the dungeon (see page 19) into the slot and presses the numbers written on the scrap of paper he found with it. This makes the lift work. "They" think he is Horace because the card is in Horace's name.

Pages 30-31

The east turret door is blue. (If you turn the page round so you can look at the map in the direction of east, you will see the view more clearly.)

Pages 32-33

Here is the pieced together Will:

THE WILL

THIS IS THE LAST WILL AND TESTAMENT OF GRANDFATHER BLOOD I HEREBY LEAVE MY SNOOKER TABLE, MY COLLECTION OF ANTIQUE SILVER SAFETY PINS AND MY JUKE BOXES TO MY SON SPIKE, MY WOODEN LEG TO HERBERT, MY DIVING GEAR AND HARPOON COLLECTION TO ARTHUR, MY PIRANHA BIRD AND MY PINBALL MACHINE TO BABY NORMAN, THE BOUND COPIES OF 'THE CROCODILE' AND 'SPIDER KEEPER'S MONTHLY' TO MATILDA AND PEARL, MY PATENT STRETCHER TO THE LOCAL HOSPITAL AND MY HOME KNOWN TO ALL AS BLOOD CASTLE, ALL MY WORLDLY WEALTH AND MY EXOTIC SNAKE COLLECTION TO MY GRANDSON BORIS.

Pages 34-35

Ivor had seen several portraits of Boris on his travels through the castle, including one in the room he is now standing in. He notices a number of differences between these and the phoney Boris standing in the doorway. The differences are ringed on this picture.

Pages 36-37

Ivor props the ladder up against the beam, threads the rope over the pulley and hooks it on to the ring of the cage. He then threads the rope through the ring again and back over the pulley. He then climbs down and pulls on the rope.

The greasiness of the ring helps to reduce the friction between it and the rope. He is just able to pull the cage up enough for Boris to crawl out. He could have threaded the rope through the ring and over the pulley a third time. In theory this would have made the cage easier to lift. However, he was worried about there being too much friction caused by the rope rubbing against itself.

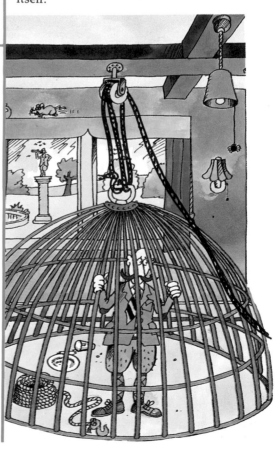

47

Pages 38-39

Ivor spotted Aunt Matilda with the crocodiles while he was looking for the lift (see page 27). He and Boris go back there to find her. (Ivor still has the card and number for operating the lift.)

They then make their way to the snake pit. They use the tin whistle Ivor found in the dungeon (page 19) to play Grandfather Blood's Little Tune to charm the snakes so they can get past them safely. (Clues to this are the pictures on the music, Boris's picture "thoughts" on page 38 and the book on "Snake Charming for Beginners" on page 8. Ivor remembers seeing the snake pit entrance when he was standing outside the castle trying to get in (pages 4-5).

Page 40

On page 13 there is a picture of Uncle Spike on the wall, tearing up some paper. If you look carefully, you will see the words on it are "The Will" in mirror writing, i.e. it is not a portrait, but a reflection in a mirror. So Uncle Spike tore up the Will.

You are probably wondering why. Well, not realizing Boris was an impostor and disgusted by his behaviour after Grandfather Blood's death, Spike thought he would destroy the Will and then try to get rid of Boris. However, you were not the only one to see him doing it. "Boris" saw him too, stole the pieces and took them to his turret room where Ivor found them.

THE CURSE OF THE LOST IDOL

Contents

About this Story

The Curse of the Lost Idol is a thrilling adventure and an intriguing mystery story set in Egypt. Keep your wits about you as you read and look carefully at the illustrations. Cryptic clues and vital evidence are lurking in the pictures and the words.

If you get stuck, there are extra clues on page 89. Remember, these are printed in a secret way. If you are still baffled and have to admit defeat, you can find all the answers, with detailed explanations on pages 90 to 96.

This is Annie. She manages to solve the mystery. Can you?

The Amazing Discovery

Professor Pott and his eager assistant, Eric, were excavating near an ancient Egyptian temple. After weeks of hot, sweaty digging they had only found boring bits of pot and a few old bones. One day, something extraordinary happened . . .

The Professor lurched forwards as the ground gave way beneath his spade.

They cleared away the loose sand to reveal a dark, gaping hole in the ground.

Eric threw a stone into the hole and waited . . . and waited to hear it fall.

Eric unravelled his handy, portable rope ladder and secured it to a large boulder. The Professor climbed gingerly down into the deep, dark hole.

Eric joined the Professor at the bottom. They were standing in an underground chamber. Eric shivered. He hoped it wasn't a tomb full of mummies.

The Professor shone his torch on the chamber walls while Eric stumbled about in the gloom.

Suddenly he collided with a cold, hard object in the middle of the chamber.

Eric grabbed the torch, expecting the worst. But he could not believe his eyes.

"A golden statue!" he squeaked in amazement. "With six toes!"

The Professor gasped and staggered. "Good grief . . . It's the lost idol!"

Even Eric knew of the lost idol . Long ago, it was said to possess mysterious, magical powers and it was worshipped throughout Ancient Egypt. 3000 years ago, the High Priest hid the idol in a secret underground chamber to protect it. Since that time many people have searched for the idol, but always in vain . . . until today.

An Ancient Curse

Eric gawped at the idol in stunned silence. He tried to lift it off the stone plinth, but his weedy biceps could not cope with the weight.

"Pure gold is very heavy," said the Professor, straining every muscle to hold the idol.

"Look! Hieroglyphics!" said Eric excitedly.

He pointed to the stone plinth on which the idol stood gleaming in the torchlight. They saw row upon row of strange pictures and intricate symbols exquisitely carved into the crumbling surface. Eric knew that centuries had passed since the last eyes had looked on the ancient message. He watched the Professor turn pale as he worked out the meaning of the mysterious symbols.

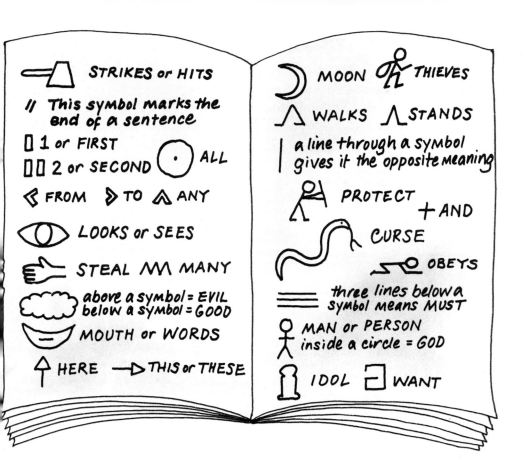

STRIKES or HITS

// This symbol marks the end of a sentence

[] 1 or FIRST

[][] 2 or SECOND

◯ ALL

⟨ FROM   ⟩ TO   ⋀ ANY

👁 LOOKS or SEES

👉 STEAL   ⋀⋀⋀ MANY

☁ above a symbol = EVIL below a symbol = GOOD

‿ MOUTH or WORDS

⬆ HERE   ⟶▷ THIS or THESE

☾ MOON   THIEVES

⋀ WALKS   ⋀ STANDS

| a line through a symbol gives it the opposite meaning

PROTECT   + AND

CURSE

OBEYS

≡ three lines below a symbol means MUST

MAN or PERSON inside a circle = GOD

IDOL   WANT

"It's a curse," said the Professor in a serious voice. "We must protect the idol. If we fail . . . who knows what might happen."

"But nothing can happen to the idol," Eric protested.

"I'm not so sure," replied the Professor. "What about the notorious Doppel Gang? They have masterminded numerous daring robberies and they go for ancient gold treasures every time. The idol is an obvious target."

"Wow!" said Eric, amazed that he could be caught up in anything so important and exciting.

"Exactly," said the Professor. "We shall have to be very careful. I must devise a plan . . . and you, Eric, must help me."

DON'T TURN THE PAGE YET

Use the Professor's notebook to work out the meaning of the curse on the stone plinth.
   What does it say?

In the News

A few days later, the Professor's fabulous discovery hit the news headlines. It caused a sensation all over the world.

Annie was fascinated by the news of the discovery and longed to see the idol. Then she spotted the competition in The Daily Wheeze. It was tricky but she puzzled out the solution. Now, perhaps, there was a chance.

DON'T TURN THE PAGE YET

Solve the Riddle of the Sphinx.

The Daily
WHEEZE

GOSSIP HEARSAY RUMOUR
We print it!

EUREKA!

POTT POTS MORE THAN A POT FOR POSTERITY

The inside story

By Sam Scoop in Cairo

Last Tuesday, deep beneath the windswept sands of the arid Egyptian desert, Professor Parsifal Pott made the discovery of a lifetime. Hardly daring to believe it, he unearthed the legendary "lost" idol – the greatest find since Tutankhamun's treasures were brought to light in 1922.

A unique treasure

The idol is no ordinary Egyptian statue. It is priceless – cast in purest gold with rare sapphires and emeralds inlaid around its head and a magnificent diamond in its back.

An ancient mystery

The idol is shrouded in mystery and magic. From its forehead rears the magic symbol of a one-eyed cobra and on its left foot there are six toes. It is also said to bear a powerful ancient curse.

Professor Pott: "I was stunned."

No idle threat

In an exclusive interview, the Professor delivered an awesome warning.

"Don't doubt the curse. It is as powerful today as it was in ancient times."

No exhibition

For these reasons, there are no plans for a public exhibition. The Professor is taking no chances. No photographs have been released and the location of the discovery site is top secret.

Potty Prof reveals all to lucky few

But! The Professor has generously offered to reveal the idol to a privileged few. Six lucky Wheeze readers will travel to Egypt to the secret site and see with their own eyes the fabulous lost idol. Solve the Riddle of the Sphinx and you stand a chance of winning this trip of a lifetime.

COMPETITION CORNER
THE RIDDLE OF THE SPHINX

The sphinx wanted to know which one of three gods stole the golden apple. Was it HORUS, ANUBIS or OSIRIS?

"I DIDN'T," said Horus. "OSIRIS DID," said Anubis.

"ANUBIS IS LYING," said Osiris.

The sphinx knew that one god was telling the truth and the other two were lying.

WHICH ONE STOLE THE GOLDEN APPLE?

Send your answer to The Daily Wheeze, Cairo Office, Egypt.

57

Annie in Egypt

Several weeks later, Annie stood in the hot sunshine pinching herself. It hurt so much she knew she wasn't dreaming. She really was in Egypt.

She rummaged in her big bag. As usual, it was bulging with a strange collection of junk including a pocket mirror, magnetic toothpick, electric torch, extra sharp penknife and a bent tin whistle. At last she found what she was searching for: her prize-winner's letter. The instructions were perplexing.

"On arrival in Egypt, the steam boat with more than than one funnel, at least 14 port side windows, a stern deck, a blue stripe but no flag will transport you up the River Nile to your secret destination. Please embark immediately."

Annie groaned as she looked at the boats moored along the quay. How many more puzzles would she have to solve? But on second thoughts, this puzzle was not so tricky. Annie raced towards the boat.

DON'T TURN THE PAGE YET

Which boat does Annie go to?

59

The Perplexing Plan

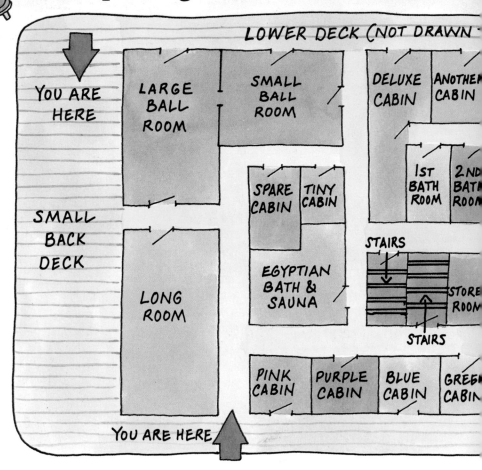

LOWER DECK (NOT DRAWN

YOU ARE HERE

LARGE BALL ROOM

SMALL BALL ROOM

DELUXE CABIN

ANOTHER CABIN

SMALL BACK DECK

SPARE CABIN

TINY CABIN

1ST BATH ROOM

2ND BATH ROOM

LONG ROOM

EGYPTIAN BATH & SAUNA

STAIRS

STORE ROOM

STAIRS

PINK CABIN

PURPLE CABIN

BLUE CABIN

GREEN CABIN

YOU ARE HERE

Annie panted up the gangplank just as the mooring ropes were cast off. There was no one in sight and Annie wondered if she had made a mistake. Where were the other passengers?

Then she heard a stomping, swooshing sound coming up behind her. She spun round to find the source of the noise

looking up at her – a little person with an enormous moustache, wearing big boots and a baggy sort of nightshirt.

"Hello, my name's Annie," she said, trying hard not to stare at his outsize moustache. "What should I do next?"

"Join the others," he squeaked. "Go along the deck, take the first

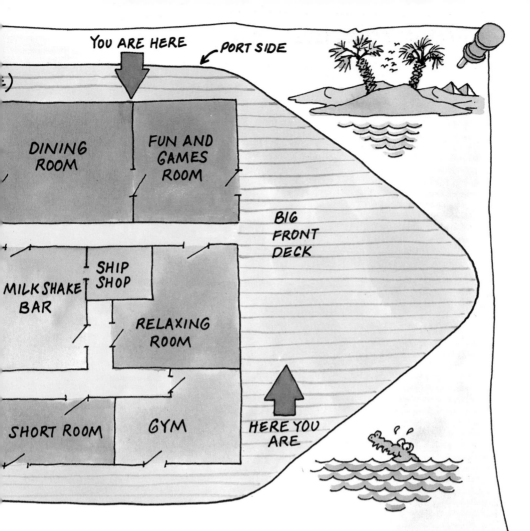

YOU ARE HERE

PORT SIDE

DINING ROOM

FUN AND GAMES ROOM

BIG FRONT DECK

SHIP SHOP

MILK SHAKE BAR

RELAXING ROOM

SHORT ROOM

GYM

HERE YOU ARE

corridor on the left, second passage on the right, turn right, turn left and left again, first right and it's the first door on the left.'' And then he scurried away.

Annie gulped, hoping she would remember the instructions. Then she spotted a boat plan, pinned to a lifebelt. It was hopeless. There were four arrows indicating YOU ARE HERE.

She stared hard at the plan for a moment or two. Then she smiled.

DON'T TURN THE PAGE YET

This is the boat plan .
   Where is Annie?
   Which room should she go to and what is her route?

Who's Who?

Annie knew she had found the right room. It was full of people talking at the tops of their voices. Annie's heart sank. They were a very odd lot and one or two looked distinctly suspicious.

Annie slunk into a corner sipping a delicious Nile Nectar cocktail. On a small table, she noticed a sheet of thick notepaper. It was a passenger list. What made it interesting were the cryptic comments beside each name.

Trying hard not to stare, Annie began fitting the names on the list with the faces in the room. It wasn't too difficult, but one thing puzzled her . . . apart from the waiters, there was one name missing.

DON'T TURN THE PAGE YET

You can see the passenger list below.
Fit the names to the faces.
Whose name is missing?

Passenger list

Annie — inquisitive and good at puzzle solving

Devilla de Visp — very fond of gold jewellery

Dr Boffin — expert on Egyptian idols

Terry Trubble — ex bank robber with a stutter

Luigi Macaroni — suspicious character with an Italian accent

Drusilla P. Culia — ancient curses fanatic – wears strange flowery clothes

Professor Pott — _brilliant_ archaeologist

Sam Scoop — Daily Wheeze reporter - does anything for a good newspaper story

Harriet Flash — Daily Wheeze photographer - good friend of Sam Scoop

63

The Mysterious Message

That night, Annie lay awake in her narrow cabin bunk, listening to the water lapping against the sides of the boat. Every so often she thought she heard a chomping noise. Crocodiles? Impossible. There weren't any crocodiles in the river – were there?

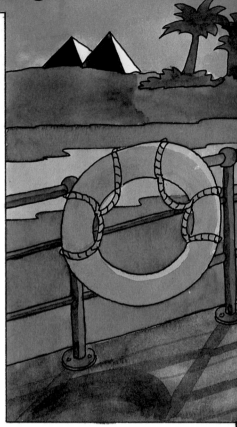

But she could definitely hear something. This time there was a clumping sound as well. It was the sort of noise made by someone wearing boots that are far too big.

Annie decided to investigate. She crept to the door in bare feet and took a deep breath ready to face whatever monster lurked outside. Then she pushed against the door with all her might.

The door flew open with a loud crash. Annie heard a high pitched squeal as she lunged into the little person with a lopsided moustache. He was chewing a very sticky toffee.

"I'm very sorry, Mr . . ." Annie said, feeling very embarassed.

The little person said nothing. He rearranged his moustache and pointed at an envelope lying on the deck.

Annie was puzzled. She opened the envelope cautiously and examined the contents. It contained a hand-drawn map and a crumpled scrap of paper. Annie read its mysterious message – it wasn't easy. She didn't really believe the message. It seemed too silly for words.

DON'T TURN THE PAGE YET

What does the message say?

tHe idle is in GRAAtE   daanjer. a
Bunch of rooFLEss krooks Aree After
it aND i aM wurrid. rimember me
thE kerss oF tHe idle..... iT will

tAKe itz rivENdj. kip yoR eyes oppen
and be wair. trust noone. GUD LUK

p.s. here is a map. it mite bee usful – you
        nerver no.

Inside the Buried Chamber

The next day, Annie and all the other passengers (except for the nameless one) set off for the buried chamber.

Professor Pott led them off the boat along a dusty path into the desert. It was baking hot and Annie longed to stop at one of the refreshment stands beside the road. In the distance she saw some rocky hills and wondered how much further it was. She panted on, passing ruins on her left and an oasis on her right. Further on, they took a left turn and came to a building surrounded by fallen masonry. This was the Temple of the Moon God. Just beyond it was the entrance to the buried chamber.

Annie made the perilous descent down the rope ladder into the buried chamber. She gazed at the smooth, flat, walls covered in paintings. She was surprised by the soft sandy floor.

Then she saw the idol – gleaming in the gloomy light. The Professor told everyone to stand back. Dr Boffin pulled out his magnifying glass and was about to examine the idol when . . .

. . . all of a sudden, the chamber was plunged into total darkness. Disembodied screams of shock rang out through the blackness. Annie could see nothing so she listened instead. She heard the Professor's voice and in the background there was a strange, scraping, digging sound.

Suddenly, without warning, the light came back. All at once, Annie knew something was wrong . . . very wrong. The idol was missing!

With a sickening jolt, Annie remembered the mystery message. Too late. Drusilla broke the awful silence with a wail and panic broke out as everyone rushed for the ladder. Annie thought fast. Was there anything she could do? There was only one thing. Hastily, she took a few snaps with her Instantpic camera. Maybe they would contain clues that would lead to the thief.

Sandstorm!

At the top of the shaft everything was dark – not pitch black, but thick and murky. A vicious wind was blowing and Annie's skin was stung by sharp grains of flying sand. The wind had suddenly whipped up a fierce sandstorm.

Annie could not see much – just a few shadowy figures. But she heard something that sent an icy shiver down her spine. Right next to her, a man and a woman were speaking in hoarse whispers. As she heard the man speak, she knew she was listening to the voice of whoever had stolen the idol. Both voices were familiar. They were passengers on the boat, but she didn't know exactly who they belonged to.

The thief said no more. Instead she heard the others, all talking at once. The Professor was urging everyone not to panic and Drusilla was wailing as usual. In addition, Annie definitely identified the voices of two other passengers. That left just four passengers as possible suspects.

DON'T TURN THE PAGE YET

**Whose voices did Annie identify?
Who are the possible suspects?**

H-h-he-help. I d-d-don't like s-s-sandstorms.
The curse! The curse! The ancient gods have sent this storm to curse us all.
Most unusual and very peculiar. Perhaps it's the curse at work.
Be quiet. Stop wittering. Ouch! This sand hurts.
Ma che scemo! Mama mia!
It's all right . . . Don't panic . . . It's just a sandstorm . . . Keep calm . . . Follow me.

Interrogation

Annie followed the Professor's voice back to the boat. She half expected to find one of the passengers missing but they were all there and not one of them looked guilty. So the thief had not made a getaway. Why not?

Ahmed Ablunda, the local Police Chief, arrived and put everyone under boat arrest. Annie found it all quite exciting – she had never been a suspect before.

Annie couldn't wait to be interrogated. She was itching to tell the police chief what she had heard. But when her turn came, he did not seem at all interested.

Instead, he asked her silly, meaningless questions. . . . Where is the Baron? What is the number of the Swiss bank account? Where is the golden mask, the doubloons and the pieces of eight?

Annie decided he was a useless detective and probably half mad. She was closer to solving the mystery than he was, so she would do some snooping on her own. But did he have any information that would help her?

Then she spotted a piece of yellow paper destined for the rubbish bin. It was covered in the Police Chief's strange scrawl. Was it Arabic? No!

She waited for a moment when he wasn't looking, picked something out of her bag and used it to decipher the scrawl. She was not sure if it was useful or not. Still, it might come in handy later.

DON'T TURN THE PAGE YET

What did Annie take out of her bag?
What is written on the yellow paper?

Footprints in the Sand

Back in her cabin, Annie tried to piece together the clues she had gathered. But they didn't make sense at all and thinking about them gave her brain ache. Then a brilliant thought struck her. The photos! Perhaps they would help.

Annie picked out one of the photos taken just after the idol vanished. Around the empty stone block were four sets of fresh footprints.

Annie's brain started to work at double speed . . . Whoever took the idol must have been near the block – close enough to lift the idol off it. So one set of footprints must belong to the thief.

Annie was very impressed by her brilliant bit of brain work. But how could she discover whose footprints they were? She worked out an ingenious plan.

After supper, Annie left the other passengers playing Egyptian snakes and ladders and crept along the corridor towards the cabins. Just as she expected, they had all left their day shoes outside their doors to be cleaned. Swiftly and silently, she crept between the cabins, checking each pair of shoes against the photo she clutched in her hand.

At the end of her search, she knew that at last she was close to finding the thief.

DON'T TURN THE PAGE YET

Whose shoes made the prints?

72

**PROFESSOR POTT'S
DESERT BOOTS**

**DRUSILLA'S
FLIP-FLOPS**

**LUIGI MACARONI'S
WINKLE PICKERS**

TERRY TRUBBLE'S TRAINERS

SAM SCOOPS SNEAKERS

HARRIET'S SPIKEY BOOTS

DEVILLA'S STILETTOS

ANNIE'S BASEBALL BOOTS

DR BOFFIN'S BROGUES

Photo Clues

Annie sneaked back to her cabin feeling very pleased with herself. She had narrowed down the list of suspects. Now another mystery began to bug her. She wanted to know what had become of the idol. Where was it?

The idol was much too big and bulky to slip into a pocket. In fact it would be impossible to remove it from the chamber hidden anywhere – in a bag, under a jacket, inside a shirt – without it showing. Unless . . .

Two photos caught her eye. They were both taken in the panic after the idol had vanished. Annie stared hard at them. Something puzzled her. Something about the chamber was wrong, or different from the way she remembered it.

In a flash Annie knew exactly where the idol was. She must go and investigate IMMEDIATELY!

DON'T TURN THE PAGE YET

Where is the idol?

Back to the Chamber

But Annie couldn't leave straight away. The other passengers started playing moonlit deck quoits right outside her cabin. So she waited until everyone had gone to bed.

She crept out on to the deck trying hard to avoid Ahmed Ablunda's men. To her dismay, the gangplank was guarded. A dozy policeman slouched against the railing, but his dog was wide awake and growling.

Annie had a brainwave. She hopped over the railing with her bag of junk and slid down a mooring rope to the shore.

Once she was on dry land, Annie looked at the moonlit landscape. Which way was the buried chamber?

Annie had a second brainwave. She rummaged in her bag for the map the man with the moustache had given her. The buried chamber was not marked and she did not know where the boat was moored. Then she remembered her journey earlier that day. Now she knew how to get there.

DON'T TURN THE PAGE YET

Where is the chamber and what is Annie's route?

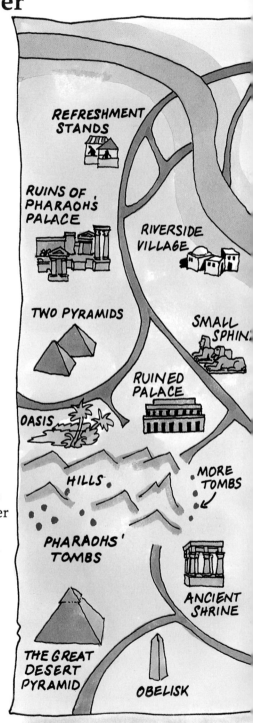

REFRESHMENT STANDS

RUINS OF PHARAOH'S PALACE

RIVERSIDE VILLAGE

TWO PYRAMIDS

SMALL SPHIN.

RUINED PALACE

OASIS

MORE TOMBS

HILLS

PHARAOHS' TOMBS

ANCIENT SHRINE

THE GREAT DESERT PYRAMID

OBELISK

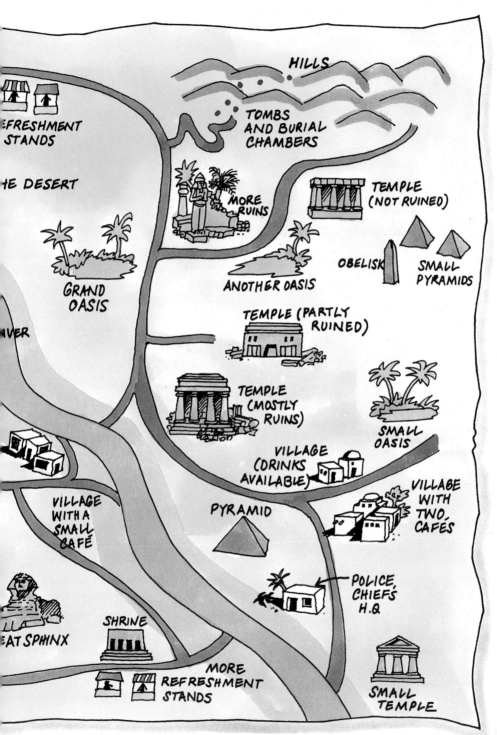

HILLS

REFRESHMENT STANDS

THE DESERT

TOMBS AND BURIAL CHAMBERS

MORE RUINS

TEMPLE (NOT RUINED)

GRAND OASIS

ANOTHER OASIS

OBELISK

SMALL PYRAMIDS

...VER

TEMPLE (PARTLY RUINED)

TEMPLE (MOSTLY RUINS)

SMALL OASIS

VILLAGE (DRINKS AVAILABLE)

VILLAGE WITH TWO CAFÉS

VILLAGE WITH A SMALL CAFÉ

PYRAMID

POLICE CHIEF'S H.Q

GREAT SPHINX

SHRINE

MORE REFRESHMENT STANDS

SMALL TEMPLE

The Crooks Return

Inside the buried chamber, Annie found the idol exactly where she thought it would be. All of a sudden, she heard a noise at the top of the shaft. Horrified, she recognized the voice of the thief speaking to his accomplice. Annie had to think fast. She must protect the idol at all costs!

She grabbed it and shoved it into her big bag – she was surprised how light it felt. Then she pressed herself against the wall hoping to hide in the gloom. She kept perfectly still. She heard two voices talking in hoarse whispers and she could just make out two shadows creeping across the chamber. Then she heard someone scrabbling frantically in the sand. They were looking for the idol! She knew she had to make a dash for it before the crooks discovered the idol was missing.

Too late! As Annie clambered up the first few rungs of the ladder, she felt a strong hand grasp her leg. She tried to grab it and push it away but she got a head instead – she felt hair, an ear and something sharp that scratched her hand. Then suddenly she was free. The thief must have lost his balance.

There was no time to lose. She had to stop the thief escaping, but he was already starting to climb the ladder. Could she trap him in the chamber? The knots securing the ladder were too tight to undo and she couldn't budge the boulder. She could cut the ropes but there was nothing sharp lying around that she could see. In the nick of time, Annie knew she was being thick. Of course she could trap him.

DON'T TURN THE PAGE YET

How does Annie trap the thief?

The Mystery Thickens

As Annie made her way back to the boat, she began to feel frightened. She tried to pull herself together – but she knew she wasn't just being silly. It really was very scary scrambling across a strange desert all alone in the middle of the night carrying a priceless idol.

And what about the curse? Annie hoped that the powers of the ancient gods would not mistake her for the thief and punish her. She started to run.

By the time she reached the gangplank, she was too exhausted to worry about the guards. She only remembered them when she passed the policeman and his dog, both fast asleep.

She made straight for her cabin and bolted the door. She knew she ought to take the idol straight to the Police Chief, but first she wanted to look at it herself. As she lifted it from her bag, something in the back of her mind worried her. What was it?

She turned it round slowly, looking at it from every angle – front, back and from both sides. The more she stared at it, the more it bothered her. In a flash she realized what was wrong. It could only mean one thing . . .

She had to act fast. Should she go to the Police Chief? No, not yet. He may not accept her story and he would waste valuable time.

80

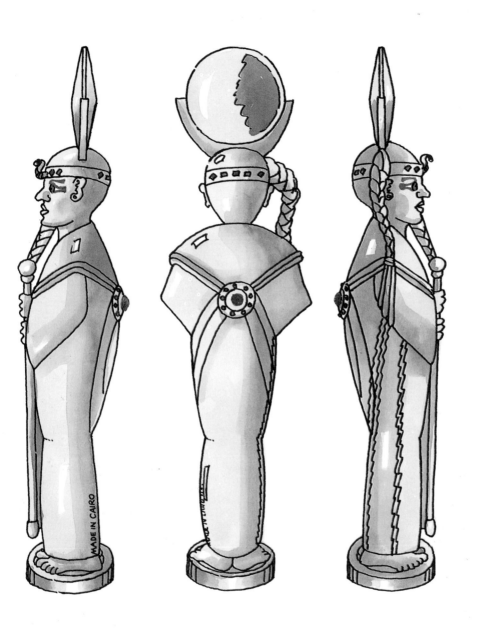

Annie racked her brains. Who could she trust? The Professor! He was sure to believe her story. She set off for his cabin.

DON'T TURN THE PAGE YET

What is wrong with the idol?
What does this mean?

In the Professor's Cabin

The Professor's door was unlocked. She nervously poked her head round the door frame and peeped inside, expecting to see the Professor fast asleep. But he was nowhere to be seen.

His cabin was not exactly empty. It was crammed from floor to ceiling with the most incredible collection of junk. There was nowhere to sit – not even on the floor, so she just stood gaping at the Professor's peculiar possessions.

Then she saw something that made her go weak at the knees. Could it be? At first she refused to believe her eyes. She looked again and this time she was certain she was staring straight at it.

Annie didn't know what to think. She slumped on to the Professor's bunk, on top of all the rubbish, feeling very, very miserable. This spoilt everything. All her cunning detective work and all her brilliant theories were wrong . . . or were they?

DON'T TURN THE PAGE YET

What did Annie spot amongst the Professor's belongings?

The Professor's Story

Just then, the Professor bounced into the room followed by the little person with the moustache. Annie jumped up, suddenly feeling very brave.

"YOU stole it," she shouted at the Professor, in her fiercest voice.

For a moment, the Professor looked puzzled. Then, instead of looking guilty or frightened, he smiled and began to explain.

"No, I didn't steal it, I'm looking after it. You must believe me. I knew the idol was in danger and so I had a copy made. I am bound by the curse to protect the idol. Who knows what might have happened otherwise."

Annie was confused. Was he telling the truth? She felt certain that he was, so she told him the whole story.

"I told you she was clever," the little person squeaked

"Well done," said the Professor slapping Annie heartily on the back. "The Police Chief has drawn a complete blank but you've already trapped the Doppel Gang!"

"The what?" spluttered Annie.

SILAS 'SPIKEY' SCARFACE

Known to be an expert thief but no criminal record so far. Left leg is shorter than right leg.

JOHN SMITH (alias Angus McHaggis, Michel Paté and Hans Sauerkraut.) A genius at foreign languages and accents. This man is ruthless.

The Professor produced an impressive looking police file and pulled out six official documents.

"The Doppel Gang," said the Professor pointing at the documents. "These are the crooks

EUSTACE WHIMPE

Very short and skinny. Has a constantly bad cough and a weedy voice. Whines a lot.

GLORIA GOLDFINGER

Tall, slim and vain. Hair colour changes often. Fond of expensive jewellery. Thought to be the brains of the gang.

DORIS DANE-JURASS

A schoolgirl - the youngest member of the gang. Crafty and cunning but looks innocent. Sometimes wears a wig.

BARON GRABBITT

Gang leader. A power crazy, highly dangerous millionaire. His home, Grabbitt Castle, is probably the gang's H.Q.

who are after the idol."

Annie stared at the documents. Her heart sank. She recognized two of the crooks as passengers on the boat. But were they the thieves?

DON'T TURN THE PAGE YET

Which members of the Doppel Gang are disguised as passengers on the boat?

The Truth at Last!

Having picked out the Doppel Gang members, Annie and the Professor went to the Police Chief. This time he DID believe her – the Professor made sure of it .

Then things started happening very quickly. Almost before she knew it, Annie was setting off once more for the buried chamber. This time she was on official police business which meant she travelled by camel.

Annie found camel riding rather tricky. She was trying hard to balance when she noticed her hand – the one she had scratched in her struggle with the thief. It was marked with blue pen.

At the same time, the uncomfortable rolling movement of the camel jolted her brain into action. At last, all the clues slotted into place. She knew for sure that she had been right all along.

Then Annie caught sight of two figures at the entrance to the chamber.

"The crooks! They've escaped," shrieked the police chief. "Stop them at once!"

There was a lot of noise as the police struggled with the crooks. Only when they were handcuffed was Annie's voice heard.

"They're not the ones. The thief and his accomplice are still in the chamber. I know who did it and I know why."

DON'T TURN THE PAGE YET

Is Annie right?
   Who is the thief and why did he do it?
   Who is his accomplice?

Afterwards

Reluctantly, the Police Chief listened to Annie's protests. He dismounted his camel rather clumsily and shuffled towards the hole in the ground. From the bottom of the shaft came the noise of desperate, muffled whispers.

By this time it was completely light and the wind was starting to blow. In the distance, Annie saw an ominous sandy cloud. Another sandstorm?

All of a sudden a vicious gust of wind blew Annie to the ground. As she struggled to her feet, she screamed in horror.

"LOOK OUT!" she yelled to the Police Chief.

The big boulder that Annie had been unable to budge was rolling towards the Police Chief. He threw himself clear only just in time. A split second later it would have squashed him flat.

Annie watched in disbelief. The boulder had stopped, lodged in the hole leading down to the chamber. The entrance to the chamber was sealed and the crooks were trapped inside.

"But that boulder weighs tons," Annie thought aloud. "It's impossible. How did it happen? Was it the wind . . . ?"

"Or the CURSE," said the Professor seriously. "The ancient gods have taken their revenge."

Everyone turned and stared at the Professor in stunned silence. Was it true? Was it really the ancient curse punishing the thief? Annie did not want to believe it, but there seemed to be no other explanation.

Afterwards, when Annie's adventure in Egypt was over, there was still one other thing that puzzled her. Who was the little person with the outsize moustache?

Do you know?

Clues

Page 54

Match the symbols in the Professor's notebook with those on the stone block. You will need to add a few small words (such as a, the, of and who) for the curse to make sense in English.

Page 56

Test each god's answer in turn and see if it is possible for that one to be telling the truth while the other two are lying.

Hint: When one god is lying accuses another, second, god of lying, it means this second god must be telling the truth.

Page 58

The port side is the left side of a boat and the stern is the back. The front of a boat is more pointed than the back. A boat with a stern deck may have other decks as well.

Page 60

Try following the instructions from each starting point. You do not need to go in the direction of the arrows.

Page 62

The clues lie in the scribbled notes. Have a good look at what people are saying and the clothes they are wearing.

Page 64

This is easy but the spelling is awful.

Page 68

There are two clues in the text. The scribbled notes on the passenger list might help (see page 62).

Page 70

The Police Chief writes from right to left. Look on page 58 to find out what Annie keeps in her bag.

Page 72

Look very carefully at the soles of the shoes. Take special notice of studs, grooves and ridges. Think what sort of print they would make.

Page 74

No one is holding or concealing the idol. Could it be hidden somewhere else? Pages 66-67 and 70-71 may give you some clues.

Page 76

Look on page 66 for the landmarks Annie passed. The pictures on page 52 may help you to pinpoint the entrance to the chamber.

Page 78

Think of the things Annie keeps in her bag (see page 58).

Page 80

Compare the idol with its description in The Daily Wheeze on page 57. Sapphires are blue and emeralds are green.

Page 82

This is easy. Use your eyes.

Page 84

Look at features which are hard to alter or hide such as noses, ears and scars.

Page 86

Who carries a blue pen? Look on pages 78-79 for more clues.

Page 88

His disguise isn't very good. His hair, glasses and squeaky voice give him away.

Answers

Pages 54-55

Here you can see what the curse means in English.

Here stands (the) idol (of the) moon god. Many evil men want (to) steal (the) idol. (The) first man (who) sees (the) idol must protect (the) idol from evil men. (A) curse strikes all thieves and any man (who) disobeys these words.

Pages 56-57

Horus stole the golden apple. Horus and Anubis were lying. Osiris was telling the truth.

Pages 58-59

The SS CHAOS is the only boat that fits the description.

Pages 60-61

Annie goes to the Long Room. The black line shows the route she takes.

Annie starts here.

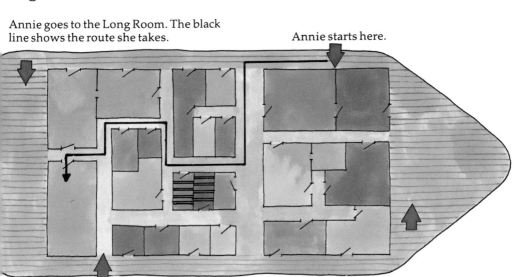

Pages 62-63

Here are the names of the passengers on the boat.

Professor Pott

Dr Boffin

Drusilla P. Culia

Terry Trubble

Harriet Flash

This person's name is missing.

Devilla de Visp

Luigi Macaroni

Sam Scoop

The waiters are the ones wearing hats like this.

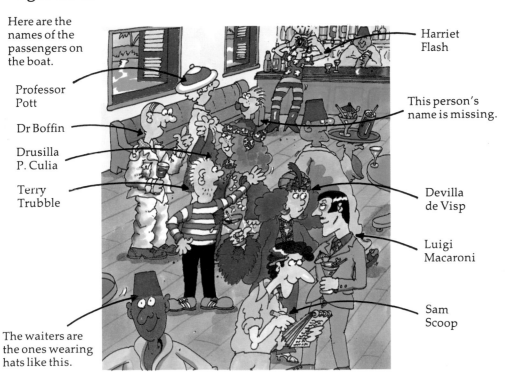

Pages 64-65

With the spelling corrected, the message says:

THE IDOL IS IN GREAT DANGER. A BUNCH OF RUTHLESS CROOKS ARE AFTER IT AND I AM WORRIED. REMEMBER THE CURSE OF THE IDOL ... IT WILL TAKE ITS REVENGE. KEEP YOUR EYES OPEN AND BEWARE. TRUST NO ONE. GOOD LUCK.

P.S. HERE IS A MAP. IT MIGHT BE USEFUL. YOU NEVER KNOW.

Pages 68-69

Annie recognizes the voices of Professor Pott, Drusilla P. Culia, Luigi Macaroni and Terry Trubble. These four can be ruled out as suspects. This leaves Dr Boffin, Sam Scoop, Devilla de Visp and Harriet Flash as possible suspects.

It's all right ... Don't panic! ... It's just a sandstorm ... Keep calm ... Follow me.

The Professor – Annie recognized his voice urging everyone not to panic.

Ma che scemo! Mama mia!

Luigi Macaroni – his Italian gives him away.

The curse! The curse! The ancient gods have sent this storm to curse us all.

Drusilla. – Annie heard her wailing as usual, just as she did in the chamber.

H-h-he-help. I d-d-don't like s-s-sandstorms.

Terry Trubble – he has a terrible stutter.

Pages 70-71

The Police Chief's notes are written back to front and the piece of paper is upside down. Annie takes her pocket mirror from her bag to read the notes (see page 58). She turns the paper the other way up and holds it in front of the mirror. Do the same thing and you can find out what is written on the yellow paper.

Pages 72-73

The footprints in the sand were made by Professor Pott, Luigi Macaroni, Sam Scoop and Dr Boffin. This means that one of these four is the thief.

Professor Pott's boot prints

Luigi Macaroni's winkle-picker prints

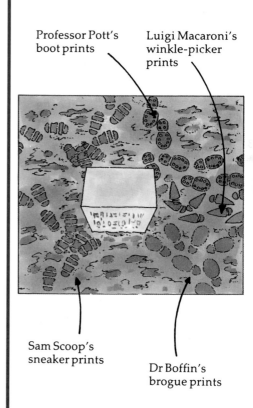

Sam Scoop's sneaker prints

Dr Boffin's brogue prints

Pages 74-75

The idol is still in the chamber. No one could have taken the idol out of the chamber as the photographs show that no one is holding or concealing it. In the suspicious conversation on page 68, the thief reveals that he does not have the idol on him.

The idol is buried in the sandy floor. Annie heard the thief doing this when the lights went out (see page 67). So did Devilla de Visp (see page 71).

The idol is buried under this mound.

Pages 76-77

The black line shows Annie's route from the river to the chamber. The entrance is in a direct line with two pyramids and an obelisk (see page 52).

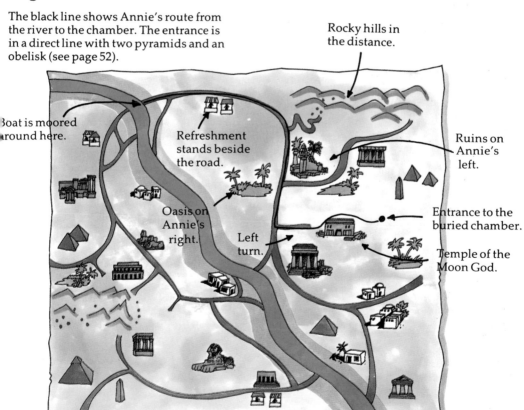

Rocky hills in the distance.

Boat is moored around here.

Refreshment stands beside the road.

Ruins on Annie's left.

Oasis on Annie's right.

Left turn.

Entrance to the buried chamber.

Temple of the Moon God.

Pages 78-79

Annie cuts the ropes at the top of the ladder with her extra strong penknife. She always carries this in her bag (see page 58).

The thief climbing up falls back down the shaft with the ladder and is trapped in the chamber.

Pages 80-81

There are four differences between the idol and the description in The Daily Wheeze (see page 57). It is much lighter than the real idol. Professor Pott

and Eric notice how heavy it is but Annie is surprised by how light it is. The modern factory stamp shows it must be a fake.

Jewels around the idol's head should be sapphires (blue) and emeralds (green).

Cobra symbol should only have one eye.

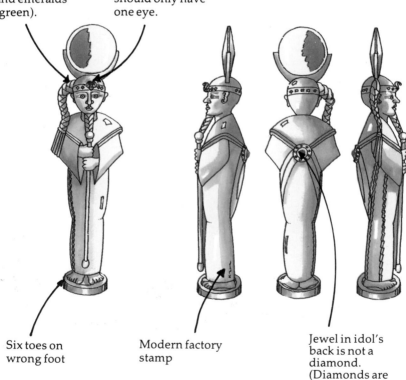

Six toes on wrong foot

Modern factory stamp

Jewel in idol's back is not a diamond. (Diamonds are not red)

Annie spots the idol half hidden beneath the lampshade on the chest of drawers. It is recognizable by the six toes on its left foot and the moon disk on its head which is just visible at the top of the shade.

The two crooks are John Smith, disguised as Luigi Macaroni and Gloria Goldfinger, disguised as Devilla de Visp.

Ahmed Ablunda must have thought that Annie was Doris Dane-Jurass in disguise (see page 70). In fact they are quite different.

He has dyed his brown hair black.

Scar on left cheek.

Shape of nose is distinctive and hard to disguise.

No moustache usually. He has grown one as a disguise.

Button nose.

Same gold earrings and necklace.

She has changed her hair colour, but it is the same style and length.

Pages 86-87

The thief is Sam Scoop. A series of clues leads Annie to discover this.

In the sandstorm (see page 68), Annie does not recognise his voice. This means he could have held the suspicious conversation and makes him a suspect alongside Dr Boffin, Deville de Visp and Harriet Flash. Annie rules out the two women because she knows the thief is a man. Annie identifies four sets of footprints (see page 72). She dismisses Professor Pott and Luigi Macaroni as suspects because she recognized their voices in the sandstorm. This leaves just two suspects: Dr Boffin and Sam Scoop.

When Annie returns to the chamber (see page 78); she hears the thief telling his accomplice that he stole the idol because it would make a good story. Annie remembers the cryptic comment beside Sam Scoop's name on the passenger list (see page 62). Now she definitely suspects Sam Scoop and not Dr Boffin.

When she discovers the real idol in the Professor's cabin and identifies the members of the Doppel Gang, Annie's theories are thrown into confusion. But not for long. While riding the camel, she notices the blue mark (see page 86). She remembers her struggle with the thief. She grabbed his head and scratched her hand on something sharp. Sam Scoop always carries a blue pen behind his ear.

Harriet Flash is Sam Scoop's accomplice. Annie knows the accomplice is a woman. She rules out Drusilla immediately because she recognizes her voice in the sandstorm (see page 68). This leaves Devilla and Harriet. When Sam Scoop returns to the chamber (see page 78), he calls his accomplice "Harry". In the gloom, Harriet's boot is just visible. These clues, plus the fact that Harriet is a good friend of Sam Scoop (see page 62), make Annie suspect Harriet. She cannot be certain until she sees Devilla, the other suspect, captured by the police at the chamber entrance (see page 86).

Page 88

It's Eric. He disguised himself and was not named on the passenger list to assist the Professor and to do some snooping in case of a theft. Eric knew Annie since they are in the same class at school. He also knew that Annie was a brilliant puzzle solver and reckoned she would be very useful if the idol really was in danger. In fact, Annie solved the mystery long before Eric even came close.

MURDER
ON THE
MIDNIGHT PLANE

Contents

About this Story

Murder on the Midnight Plane is a sinister story of death in the air, a gang of crooks and buried treasure. The Sprockett twins, shown in the picture below, are innocent passengers on the ill-fated plane. Between them, they unravel the mystery and uncover the killer. Now see if you can do the same.

If you get stuck, there are extra clues on page 137. If you are completely stumped, you will find all the answers, with explanations, on pages 138 to 144.

Spike Sprockett

Sam Sprockett

At the Airport

The Sprockett twins, Sam and Spike, gazed down at the bustling confusion of Capitol City International Airport.

At last their holiday had begun and they were off to join their Uncle Tom in his search for buried treasure on Tsetse, one of the exotic Los Mosquitos islands.

Neither Spike nor Sam had ever flown in a plane before and they were both feeling more apprehensive than they dared to admit.

Spike looked at his watch. It was eight o'clock which meant their plane was due to leave in exactly one hour's time.

"What do we do now?" asked Spike, hoping he sounded cooler than he felt.

"Go to the check-in desk of course," said Sam, trying to sound like an experienced air-traveller. "But I haven't a clue which one."

Spike sat on his case and stared through the railings. There were ten check-in desks.

"I think I know which one we want," he said. "Follow me."

DON'T TURN THE PAGE YET

Which check-in desk should they go to?

In the Departure Lounge

Half an hour later, the twins were slurping banana milkshakes in the departure lounge.

Spike was making gurgling noises with his straw, when he noticed someone standing beside him, reading a book about aeroplanes. Spike looked up and to his surprise, saw Barney, the boy who lived up the road.

"What are you doing here?" Spike spluttered.

Barney started to explain that he was off to Tsetse to see his granny, when an announcement boomed over the public address system.

"SWATAIR REGRET TO ANNOUNCE DELAYS OF THREE AND FOUR HOURS TO FLIGHTS SW 013 AND SW 015 RESPECTIVELY..."

There was a long wait ahead. Sam studied the strange collection of people in the departure lounge and listened. One by one she picked out the other passengers bound for Tsetse.

DON'T TURN THE PAGE YET

Which passengers are travelling to Tsetse?

That's our flight, Max. Now we're leaving at midnight.

How interesting . . . this book says that every plane which flies to Tsetse has just two propellers and carries up to 13 passengers.

103

Plane Spotting

It was nearly midnight. At last, their plane was ready for take-off. Sam and Spike ran along the maze-like corridors towards departure gate 13.

Suddenly, they found themselves in a long, dimly-lit room with an enormous window. They stopped to look out on to the floodlit tarmac below.

"I wonder which plane will take us to Tsetse," said Sam, thinking aloud.

Spike looked puzzled. He wished he had Barney's book of aeroplanes to look at, but Barney had run on ahead. Then he realized he could spot the plane without any extra help. In fact, it was really quite easy.

DON'T TURN THE PAGE YET

Which plane will Sam and Spike be travelling on?

On to the Plane

S am glanced at her watch. They were late! She grabbed Spike's arm, yanking him away from the window, and dashed down the corridor.

Suddenly, a man stepped out of nowhere. Sam crashed straight into him, spilling the entire contents of her bag over the floor.

The man muttered something under his breath. Then he bent down and started scooping Sam's possessions back into her bag.

Sam picked herself up and started to apologize, but the man had disappeared into thin air.

Sam snatched her bag and chased after Spike, through the departure gate and out on to the tarmac.

At last, they reached the plane. They clattered up the rickety steps and into the tiny cabin.

A stewardess stumbled towards them, took a flying leap over a pile of luggage and almost landed on Spike.

"Welcome aboard," she gasped, noting down the numbers of the twins' seats from their boarding passes.

She told them to go and sit in their seats, then she thrust a thick wad of leaflets into Spike's hands and disappeared.

The twins were bewildered. First, they had to find their seats but, judging by the chaos in the cabin, this was not an easy task. Spike searched for some seat numbers, but there did not appear to be any. He asked a man with a broken leg for some help, but the man was as puzzled as Spike. Then Sam had an amazing brainwave.

Seat Search

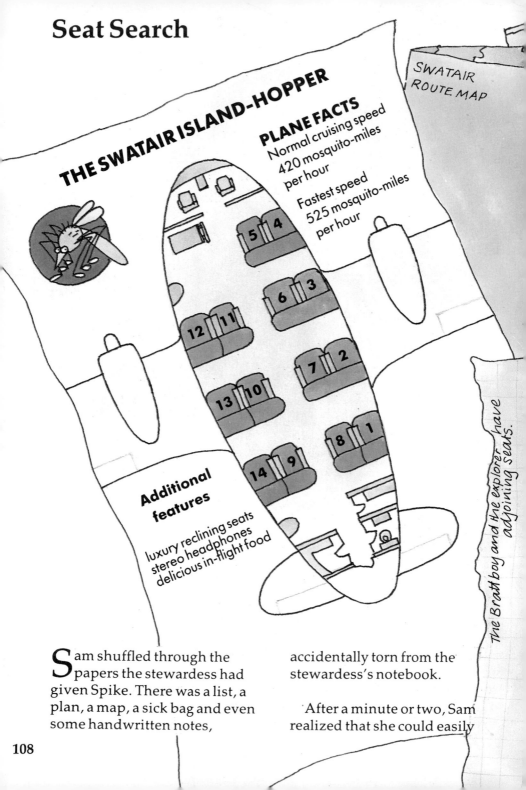

THE SWATAIR ISLAND-HOPPER

SWATAIR ROUTE MAP

PLANE FACTS
Normal cruising speed
420 mosquito-miles per hour

Fastest speed
525 mosquito-miles per hour

Additional features
luxury reclining seats
stereo headphones
delicious in-flight food

The Bratt boy and the explorer have adjoining seats.

Sam shuffled through the papers the stewardess had given Spike. There was a list, a plan, a map, a sick bag and even some handwritten notes, accidentally torn from the stewardess's notebook.

After a minute or two, Sam realized that she could easily

SWATAIR PATENT SICK BAG

B.B.N. Pole has the seat directly behind Mr Megger-Bux

Doctor Quickley sits behind Billy Bratt

Ed Banger has multi-coloured hair.

Sir Chand-Fyndes (and his pet vulture) has an aisle seat.

Mr & Mrs Megger-Bux have adjoining seats

PASSENGER LIST

PILOT Charlie Sierra
CO-PILOT off sick
STEWARDESS Dotty Fluster

Mr Max Megger-Bux
Mrs Megger-Bux
Mr Reeman
Barney B. N. Pole
Doctor Harry Quickley
Samantha Sprockett
Spike Sprockett
Pearl-Anne Plane
Christopher Wave
Sir Chand-Fyndes
Ed Banger
Billy Bratt
Inspector Ramsbottom

Mr Wave needs space for his crutches — he has 2 adjoining seats in the back row.

The doctor and the blonde lady occupy adjoining seats.

Mr Reeman has seat number 13.

No one sits in front of Mrs Megger-Bux (the pink haired lady).

Ed Banger sits directly in front of Mr Wave

Inspector Ramsbottom sits directly behind Mrs Plane.

locate their seats. What was more, she could work out where the other passengers were sitting and could even put names to their faces.

DON'T TURN THE PAGE YET

Can you match the names of the passengers with their faces and work out where each one sits?

Death in the Air

A few hours later, the Tsetse plane was well on its way, flying due south, high above the Thalassic ocean.

Inside the plane, the passengers were pinned to their seats as the in-flight movie drew to a chilling and dramatic end.

Sam peered up the gangway to see the welcome sight of the stewardess wheeling out a clanking drinks trolley.

Almost everyone jumped to life at the sound of the drinks trolley. Spike leapt out of his seat and

fought his way through a jungle of grabbing hands, wobbling bottles and spilled drinks. At last,

he grabbed two glasses of cherrycola, only just saving them from the greedy grasp of Billy Bratt.

AAAGH !

Spike was happily slurping his cherrycola when a bloodcurdling scream ripped through the plane.

The twins leapt up to find Barney looking very white and the man in front of Spike slumped half way across Barney's seat.

"Barney! What did you do to him?" yelled Sam.
"Nothing," Barney protested." I just found him like this."

I'm a doctor.

Immediately, the man from seat number three dashed down the gangway clasping a big, blue bag.

He knelt over the man and examined him with all sorts of extraordinary medical instruments.

The doctor looked grim-faced. He stood up and exclaimed in a loud, serious voice,
"This man is dead."

Was it the Food?

There was a stunned silence as the doctor laid a rug over the dead man.

"Wh...wh...what did he d..d..die of?" asked Barney, turning white.

"All the symptoms suggest food poisoning," said the doctor. "I strongly suspect that it was caused by something that the man ate for his dinner on this plane."

Spike turned a sickly shade of green as he thought back to the enormous food trolley laden with all sorts of delicious things.

Now he wished he hadn't been quite so greedy. He remembered every mouthful of gooey gateaux and greengage icecream. He could even recall everything the other passengers had eaten.

Then, in a flash of inspiration, Spike realized that he could easily use his memory to work out whether the doctor was right or not.

DON'T TURN THE PAGE YET

Was the dead man poisoned by the food he ate on the plane?

Spike Spots Something Suspicious

Spike announced his discovery in a loud voice, feeling a lot less green. Most of the other passengers seemed relieved, but the doctor just grunted and glowered at him.

All of a sudden, something caught his eye. He stared at it in horror. With a sickening jolt, he realized that if it WAS what it appeared to be, it cast an ominous shadow over the man's death.

BEFORE

What was more, Spike felt sure that he had seen it before. But where? He turned away for a split second. But when he looked back, it was gone. Had it disappeared or had someone hidden it?

DON'T TURN THE PAGE YET

These two pictures show what Spike saw before and after he looked away.

What was the suspicious thing Spike spotted?

AFTER

The Dead Man's Message

Spike wondered what to do next. Then he noticed the dead man's empty glass. He picked it up and sniffed it. Immediately, Spike knew there was something wrong.

"This tomato juice smells very strange," he said to the doctor.

But before the doctor could reply, the explorer, Sir Chand-Fyndes, pushed forwards and took the glass.

"A deceptive scent of strawberries," the explorer muttered, sniffing the glass. "This can only mean one thing . . . Akimbo poison! This man has been murdered."

There was a deathly hush. Then the man in the green overcoat walked down the gangway.

"I'm Inspector Ramsbottom," he said, flashing an identity card. "Tell me more about this poison."

"It comes from the deadly sap of the Akimbo tree," the explorer explained. "It smells sweet but kills instantly . . . and it always leaves a small ring of bright purple spots on the victim's face."

The explorer removed the dead man's hat and Sam gasped in horror. She recognized the dead man immediately.

Something in the back of her mind nagged her. Was she imagining it, or had he slipped an envelope into her bag?

Yes! There WAS an envelope! She tore it open and out fell a letter. It seemed to be written in a foreign language . . . or was it?

Iha Vevita,

Lin forma ti onfory ourun cleconcer nin G.T. Hets et setre asuret "ELL-HIMT". Hata nanci entchar (TWH), ich pinpo int St. Hetre asur, eh? Asbe enst O'LENBY agre edygan gofbo. Un tyhun tersia, mont heirtra ilbu ticanno. Ti denti? Fyth emun ti lire acht set-sew. Heret hepro ofine edawa it smeth esetre ac: HEROUS VILLA,
                    IN-SARET,
                    RAVELLI, NGW.

I thus totset SETHEY WILLS to Patnot, hing TOPRO-TEC (TT). Heirsel (fish) plansan dife arfor myli feifa nyt, hin ghappen stomep. "LE ASEF" ol lowmyc luest heywi (LLL). Eady outot hecro, OK? Sandt hent othec hartt. He rearef urt herins tructi onsrol ledu pin-prin. T.T. Akeca re Andgo.

Odlu,

C.K.

DON'T TURN THE PAGE YET

What does the letter say?

Full Speed Ahead

There was no doubt that the dead man was telling the truth. His murder was the proof. Sam looked hard at the other passengers. Which ones were the crooks? Who was the murderer? If only she could find the answer. But no one looked remotely guilty.

Sam's thoughts were abruptly interrupted by the pilot's voice booming from a loudspeaker above her head.

"Owing to an unforeseen murder, we shall now fly at full speed, on the shortest course to Tsetse, in order to arrive ahead of schedule."

Sam glanced at her watch. It was half past three and they still had to find the dead man's further instructions. How much time did they have? She looked at the map the stewardess had given Spike.

"Where are we?" she muttered.

Just then, the stewardess waltzed by and told her. They were directly above the mouth of the River Okracoke.

DON'T TURN THE PAGE YET

How much time do Sam and Spike have left on the plane to find the further instructions?

TIGERIA

LAVA LAND

139 MM

OKRACOKE RIVER

65 MM

3 HFT

181 MM

69 MM

98 MM

126 MM

81 MM

63 MM

1 3/4 HFT

112 MM

THE LOST CONTINENT

190 MM

95 MM

52 MM

160 MM

67 MM

172 MM

KEY TO MAP

——— SWATAIR PLANE ROUTES

- - - - SWATCOPTER ROUTES

● AIRPORTS   ○ JUNCTIONS

MM : MOSQUITO-MILES
HFT : HOURS OF FLYING TIME

Numbers refer to distance or flying time between nearest airport or junction

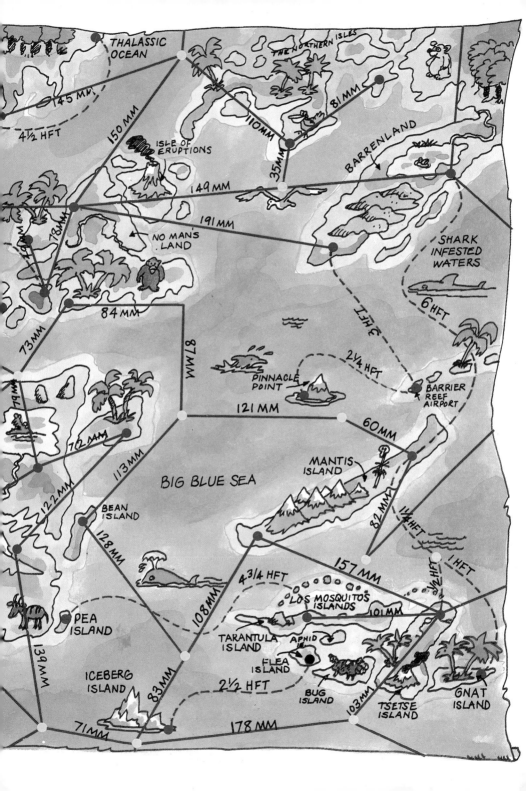

Chewy Toffees

The plane jolted into overdrive and began to climb. Immediately, Spike felt an alarming popping sensation inside his ears. Sam came up with a brilliant solution – an enormous box of chewy toffees. By now, everyone on the plane seemed to be complaining of ear popping, so Spike jumped up and passed them around.

Suddenly, something jolted his memory and he remembered where he had seen the poison bottle before. It had stood on the drinks trolley while everyone scrabbled for drinks and glasses.

How easy it must have been for the murderer to slip a few drops of poison into a glass of tomato juice. No one would have noticed, but Spike HAD noticed the hands around the trolley. What was more, he could remember each one very clearly.

If only he could work out whose hands they were, then he could draw up a list of murder suspects. In a flash of brilliance, Spike knew he could work it out. After passing round the toffees it was easy.

DON'T TURN THE PAGE YET

Who was at the drinks trolley?

121

Spike Finds the Poison Bottle

Spike slumped back down into his seat, feeling pleased with himself. Absent-mindedly, he dug his hand into the big box of chewy toffees and scrabbled around, feeling for his favourite flat, round ones.

All of a sudden, he felt something strange. It was cold and hard and not at all toffee-shaped. He looked down to investigate. He gasped when he saw it and a shiver ran down his spine. How had it dropped into the toffee box? There was only one way. The killer must have put it there while he was handing round the toffees.

He looked at the little bottle and hoped it hadn't leaked inside the toffee box. Then he realized that the poison bottle might actually lead him closer to the killer. He thought hard for a few minutes while a theory started to take shape in his mind. If he was correct, then he could narrow down the list of murder suspects even further.

DON'T LOOK AT THE OPPOSITE PAGE YET

How does Spike narrow down the list of suspects?
Which passengers are murder suspects?

Now Spike was feeling extremely pleased with himself. He even started to wonder whether the Department of Criminal Investigation might offer him a holiday job.

He was roused from his day dream by the noise from the seat in front, where Inspector Ramsbottom was sorting through the dead man's possessions. Mrs Plane was helping the Inspector. Spike noticed that she seemed very interested in the dead man's things, but he could not decide whether this was suspicious or not.

Sam peered over the top of her seat. All at once, she remembered something, but she wasn't sure quite what it was. It niggled in the back of her brain and the more she stared at the man's things, the more the niggle grew.

Then she remembered the dead man's message and everything clicked into place. Of course! Now she knew where to find the dead man's further instructions.

DON'T TURN THE PAGE YET

Where are the dead man's further instructions?

A Message in the News

MYSTERY BANK BREAK-IN

by Horace Grovell

Police are investigating a mysterious break-in at Grimbleys Bank in London.

Last Friday night, crafty thieves outwitted the bank's highly sophisticated alarm system and penetrated the steel-walled underground vaults.

Until now, the bank's computerized system of hi-security, combination locks was believed to be foolproof. Specialists assisting the police say they are stumped. So far, they have been unable to work out how the cunning crooks broke through the intricate locking system and they have no idea how the alarm mechanism was discovered and temporarily de-activated.

But the thieves were unaware of an automatic

Grimbleys Bank:
the police are stumped.

security camera, hidden in the wall of the vaults. A roll of film clearly shows the three villains inside the vault, but so far, the Police have been unable to identify them. The film has now been sent to Tsetse in the hope that someone on the island will recognize the crooks.

What makes this case so perplexing, is that nothing of any value was stolen. Bank officials report that the vault contains countless precious jewels and bank notes to the sum of many millions. But just one safe-box was opened and this contained an apparently worthless roll of parchment.

The latest news from London is that the Police have handed the case over to a mystery man, believed to be a top private detective. This mystery man is said to have his own special theory concerning the theft. When questioned, he refused to comment, saying only that it was too dangerous to divulge his discoveries while the crooks were still at large.

Unexpected security leaks at Police HQ reveal that the mystery detective is linking the Grimbley's Bank robbery with the Tsetse treasure expedition, currently headed by Thomas Sprockett in the Los Mosquitos islands. There is a suggestion that the stolen parchment is an ancient treasure chart.

S pike waited for the Inspector to look the other way, then he stretched over and took the newspaper from the seat in front.

He wasn't sure quite what to look for. He opened it and started to read. Where were the dead man's instructions? At first he wasn't

PRICELESS IDOL DISCOVERED

A fantastic, gold statue has been unearthed in Egypt. Experts believe it to be the legendary "lost idol", buried thousands of years ago under the desert sands. More news on this fabulous find in tomorrow's edition.

Singer vanishes

ED BANGER, the ex-lead singer of "Awful Noises", disappeared from his New York apartment last Thursday. He has not been seen since.

Schoolgirl's solo stunts

CHLOE, the schoolgirl stunt pilot has broken another breathtaking record in the history of aviation, by flying solo from London to Toronto in just under 12 hours.

Speedy Nik

AMATEUR SKIING ACE, Speedy Nik, astounded spectators in a death-defying down hill race in Val Despair last Saturday. On his tungsten-tipped, three metre skis, Speedy zipped through deep gulleys of powder snow and cleared a bottomless crevasse with a staggering triple-twist back-flip to pip every contestant to the post. With this victory behind him, Speedy Nik is now talking of taking up water sports.

MILLIONAIRE

MULTIMILLIONAIRE, Maximillian Megger-Bux has denied rumours that he is fleeing the country to escape the fraud squad. He was spotted yesterday making two flight reservations to an undisclosed destination. Mr Megger-Bux claims he is simply taking a short vacation in the sun.

CLASSIFIED ADS

TEA LADY required. Apply to Boris Blood, Blood Castle, San Guinaria.

WANTED: Rare books on magic and ancient curses. Write to Drusilla P. Culia. P.O. Box 666.

FOR SALE: One ostrich outfit (with feathers). Miss Putty, Tel. 675 3018.

AMAZING DUNGEON SALE. Bargain spears, handmade rat traps and much much more . . . One day only! Friday 13th, Blood Castle.

FOR SALE: Custom built, triple-fin surf board with velcro ankle-strap. Christopher Wave, 1001 Ocean Boulevard, LA.

HAIR transplant urgently needed by embarrassed school master. Genuine offers only. Tel. 243276

---

sure, but the more he looked, the more obvious it became that the dead man was trying to tell them something.

DON'T TURN THE PAGE YET

What are the dead man's instructions?

Searching the Plane

Sam and Spike were stumped. They had to find the dead man's vital information in order to hand it to Uncle Tom. But where were they supposed to start searching?

There was only one solution. Trying hard not to appear too inquisitive or suspicious, they searched every part of the plane from the galley through to the cockpit.

Half an hour later, they were almost on the point of giving up the search. Then they suddenly spotted it. Nobody noticed as Sam slipped it into the pocket of her dungarees.

DON'T TURN THE PAGE YET

These pictures show some of the places Sam and Spike searched. Where is the vital information?

127

The Landing Game

Now there was only one thing left to puzzle out. But what had the dead man meant by the "final trivial answer"? Was it a cryptic clue or even some sort of code? Spike racked his brains for inspiration and stared out of the window. With a sinking feeling, he realized they were starting their descent to Tsetse.

Sam peered round the back of Barney's seat. The stewardess was stumbling down the gangway, stopping at every row. At last she came to Sam and Spike.

"We're coming in to land now," she chirped, brightly. "I'm afraid it's going to be a very bumpy landing – it usually is with Captain Sierra at the joystick."

Spike started to feel nervous, but he hoped it didn't show. Then the stewardess handed him a card.

"Perhaps you would like to play the landing game," she said, trying to dispel Spike's obvious fears. "It might take your mind off the bumps."

Spike grimaced. Neither he nor Sam were in the mood for games, but he took the game card anyway. Sam glanced at it. Then she read the words printed at the top . . .

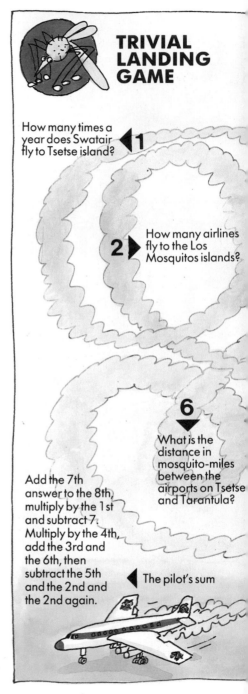

TRIVIAL LANDING GAME

How many times a year does Swatair fly to Tsetse island? **1**

2 How many airlines fly to the Los Mosquitos islands?

6 What is the distance in mosquito-miles between the airports on Tsetse and Tarantula?

Add the 7th answer to the 8th, multiply by the 1st and subtract 7. Multiply by the 4th, add the 3rd and the 6th, then subtract the 5th and the 2nd and the 2nd again.

The pilot's sum

Find the final trivial answer and you stand to win a fabulous free flight of a lifetime.

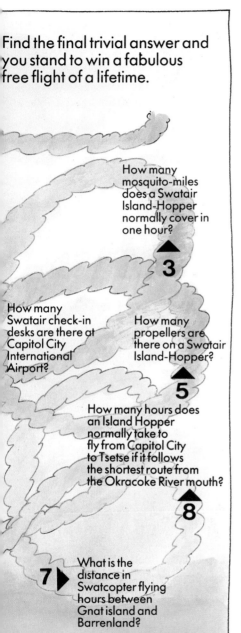

How many mosquito-miles does a Swatair Island-Hopper normally cover in one hour?

▲ 3

How many Swatair check-in desks are there at Capitol City International Airport?

How many propellers are there on a Swatair Island-Hopper?

▲ 5

How many hours does an Island Hopper normally take to fly from Capitol City to Tsetse if it follows the shortest route from the Okracoke River mouth?

▲ 8

7 ▶ What is the distance in Swatcopter flying hours between Gnat island and Barrenland?

"This is it!" she cried. "Quick! There's no time to lose."

"But how do we play this game?" asked Spike, searching for non-existent instructions.

The stewardess came to their rescue and explained.

"Follow the plane as it loops the loop towards the ground. Answer each question in turn, then work out the pilot's sum to find the final answer."

The twins worked quickly, using Spike's calculator and a lot of brain-power. Several minutes later, just as the landing wheels bounced on to the tarmac, the twins came up with the final answer.

Sam grinned from ear to ear as the plane taxied to halt. She leaned across and stared out of the window. Outside, she saw the tiny airport building and there, in the window, was Uncle Tom waiting for them. The twins leapt out of their seats in a scramble for the door and stepped out into the hot Tsetse sunshine.

DON'T TURN THE PAGE YET

**Play the landing game.
What is the final answer?**

A Perplexing Riddle

The twins threw themselves into Uncle Tom's arms and poured out the story of their flight. Then Sam thrust the yellow envelope into Uncle Tom's hands. He ripped it open and pulled out a piece of paper. On it was written a perplexing message and a riddle. At first it made no sense at all, but with a little inspiration, Uncle Tom and the twins puzzled out its meaning.

DON'T TURN THE PAGE YET

What is the meaning of this strange message?

The proof you need is waiting at the airport inside the
answer to this riddle:

MY FIRST IS IN FLYING BUT NEVER AT NIGHT
MY SECOND'S IN PILOT BUT NEVER IN FLIGHT
MY THIRD'S NOT IN TREASURE BUT IS IN THE CHART
MY FOURTH IS IN TICKET BUT NOT IN DEPART
MY FIFTH IS IN DANGER AND ALSO IN RED
MY SIXTH IS IN MURDER BUT NEVER IN DEAD

Its number is the same as my seat. I have already given
you the key that will open its door.

Proof in the Negatives

Inside the locker was yet another, bigger, yellow envelope. Uncle Tom unsealed it very carefully and gently lifted out two long strips of film. They were black and white negatives. He held them up to the light and stared at them.

"My goodness!" Uncle Tom exclaimed. "This film was taken in the vaults of Grimbleys bank. It actually shows the theft of the ancient treasure chart. It must have been taken by the bank's hidden automatic security camera."

He held up the film to let Spike and Sam have a good look. It was hard to work out what was what as dark areas were shown as light and vice versa.

"Do you recognize these criminals?" asked Uncle Tom.

"Yes, I do," cried Spike, triumphantly. "And I know where to find the treasure chart, too!"

DON'T TURN THE PAGE YET

Who are the thieves and where is the treasure chart?

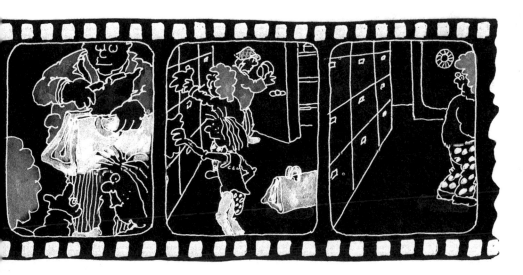

The Ancient Treasure Chart

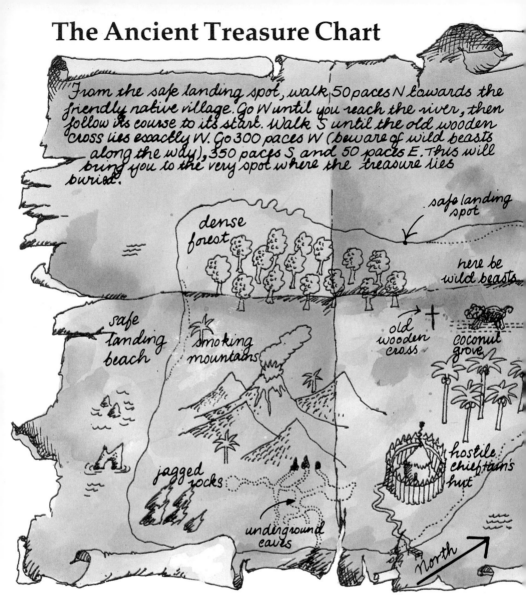

From the safe landing spot, walk 50 paces N towards the friendly native village. Go W until you reach the river, then follow its course to its start. Walk S until the old wooden cross lies exactly W. Go 300 paces W (beware of wild beasts along the way), 350 paces S and 50 paces E. This will bring you to the very spot where the treasure lies buried.

safe landing spot

dense forest

here be wild beasts

safe landing beach

smoking mountains

old wooden cross

coconut grove

hostile chieftain's hut

jagged rocks

underground caves

North

Uncle Tom dashed off in search of Inspector Ramsbottom. He left Sam and Spike sitting on a bench, crossing their fingers in the hope that the crooks hadn't made a quick getaway.

After what felt like hours, Uncle Tom returned with the Inspector. The crooks had been detained and the treasure chart rescued. Very cautiously, Uncle Tom unrolled the ancient, flaking map.

this line is the distance of 200 paces

HMS 'Honora' ran aground here 1698

Beware the quicksand

Coral reef

sinister statues

Malaria River

foul smelling swamp

Village (friendly natives)

here be dragons?

safe landing spot

galleon wrecked in storm Dec 1706

In the top left-hand corner there were some strange instructions written in ancient, spidery script. What did they mean? Then Sam had an idea and pulled out her little traveller's compass.

"I know how to find the treasure," she said.

DON'T TURN THE PAGE YET

Where is the treasure buried?

Naming the Killer

Uncle Tom rolled up the map and turned to the twins.

"Whatever would have happened if you hadn't travelled on the midnight plane?" he said. "Without you two, the Tsetse treasure would have been swiped by that bunch of unscrupulous bounty-hunters..."

"And they may never have been caught," added the detective.

Sam blushed. Then she remembered the poor man in seat number 13. Without him, they would never have been able to catch the crooks. But he was dead.

"But we still don't know who killed poor Mr Reeman," she said in a quiet voice.

Everyone was silent. Spike thought back. He remembered the drinks trolley ... the box of sweets ... the little poison bottle ... and his list of murder suspects. Slowly, the facts started to fall into place.

"But we DO know who killed him," said Spike, feeling a bit more cheerful. "It's obvious!"

DON'T TURN THE PAGE YET

Who was the killer?

136

Clues

Page 100

Have you seen the adverts on the wall? The departure times are shown using the 24 hour clock.

Page 102

Look at the flight numbers on luggage labels and boarding passes. Pay special attention to what people are saying.

Page 104

Look for the airline logo and remember what Barney said on page 102.

Page 108

The most important clues are in the stewardess's notes. Go through each clue, one by one, working out where each passenger can and cannot possibly sit. Look on pages 102-103 to find out some of the passenger's names.
Look on page 107 to find the numbers of Sam and Spike's seats.

Page 112

Did any of the passengers eat the same things as the dead man?

Page 114

This is easy. Use your eyes.

Page 116

Ignore spaces and punctuation marks.

Page 118

Look at the plane facts on page 108. Divide the speed of the plane per minute by the distance of the shortest route to Tsetse.

Page 120

Look carefully at the hands around the drinks trolley on page 110.

Page 122

If the killer dropped the poison bottle into the box, the killer must have been one of the passengers who accepted a toffee.

Page 123

Look back to the dead man's message on page 117. Where will the twins find further instructions?

Page 124

Have you noticed the dots on the newsprint?

Page 126

The message in the newspaper tells you what to look for. Use your eyes.

Page 128

You will need to flick back through the book to find some of the answers.

Page 130

The answer to the riddle is a six letter word. Each line of the riddle gives you a clue to a letter, in the correct order. Look at the newspaper message on pages 124-125 to find the key.

Page 132

The three thieves are passengers on the plane. Look carefully at their shapes, features and hands.

Page 134

N = North, S = South, E = East, W = West.
Where is North on the map?

Page 136

Which of the thieves are on the list of murder suspects?

Answers

Pages 100-101

Sam and Spike should go to check-in desk number 8. They are flying to Tsetse on flight number SW013 at 21.00 hours (9 o'clock).

Pages 102-103

The passengers travelling to Tsetse are ringed in black. Ignore the letters for now. They are part of the answer to the puzzle on pages 108-109.

Pages 104-105

The plane that Sam and Spike will be travelling on is ringed in black. It is the only SWATAIR plane which fits Barney's description of planes that fly to Tsetse (see page 102).

Pages 108-109

Here are the names and seat numbers of each passenger. Look over the page to fit the names with the faces.

Christopher Wave	1 and 8
Ed Banger	2
Doctor Harry Quickley	3
Billy Bratt	4
Sir Chand-Fyndes	5
Pearl-Anne Plane	6
Inspector Ramsbottom	7
Sam Sprockett	9
Barney B.N. Pole	10
Mr Megger-Bux	11
Mrs Megger-Bux	12
Mr Reeman	13
Spike Sprockett	14

To fit the names of the passengers with their faces, look at the picture on page 138. Match the letters beside each passenger with the letters beside each name in the list below. For instance, passenger A is Christopher Wave, passenger B is Ed Banger etc.

A Christopher Wave
B Ed Banger
C Doctor Harry Quickley
D Billy Bratt
E Sir Chand-Fyndes
F Pearl-Anne Plane
G Inspector Ramsbottom

H Sam Sprockett
I Barney B.N. Pole
J Mr Megger-Bux
K Mrs Megger-Bux
L Mr Reeman
M Spike Sprockett

Pages 112-113

Every item of food eaten by the dead man was also eaten by at least one other passenger. Since all the other passengers are alive and well, it is unlikely that the dead man was poisoned by his food.

Pages 114-115

Spike spotted a small bottle filled with green liquid. The skull and crossbones on the label suggest the liquid is poison.

When he looked again, the bottle was covered by Pearl-Anne Plane's knitting bag.

Pages 116-117

Sam and Spike decoded the message by removing all the spaces and punctuation marks. From the meaning of the message, they were able to insert new ones.

The decoded message reads as follows:

I have vital information for your uncle concerning the Tsetse treasure. Tell him that an ancient chart, which pin-points the treasure, has been stolen by a greedy gang of bounty hunters. I am on their trail but I cannot identify them until I reach Tsetse, where the proof I need awaits me. These treacherous villains are travelling with us to Tsetse. They will stop at nothing to protect their selfish plans, and I fear for my life. If anything happens to me, please follow my clues. They will lead you to the crooks and then to the chart. There are further instructions rolled up in print. Take care and good luck.

Pages 118-119

The shortest route to Tsetse is shown below, in black. It is 945 mosquito-miles long. The fastest speed of the plane is 525 mosquito-miles per hour (see page 108). If the plane flies at this speed all the way, Sam and Spike have one hour and 48 minutes (108) minutes to find the dead man's further instructions. (This means they will arrive in Tsetse at 18 minutes past five.)

The plane is here

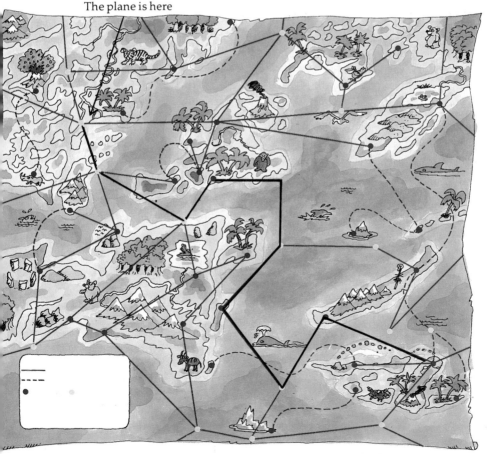

Pages 120-121

Here you can see who was standing at the drinks trolley. Any one of these people (except for the dead man) could be the murderer.

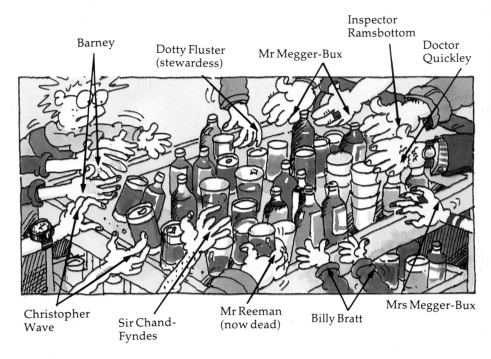

Barney

Dotty Fluster (stewardess)

Mr Megger-Bux

Inspector Ramsbottom

Doctor Quickley

Christopher Wave

Sir Chand-Fyndes

Mr Reeman (now dead)

Billy Bratt

Mrs Megger-Bux

Page 122

Spike realizes that if the killer dropped the poison bottle into the toffees, then the killer must have been one of the people who accepted a toffee. Those who refused did not put their hands into the toffee box (see pages 120-121).

Four people refused a toffee: Inspector Ramsbottom, Pearl-Anne Plane, Mrs Megger-Bux and Barney. They are struck off the list of murder suspects, leaving Christopher Wave, Doctor Quickley, Billy Bratt, Sir Chand-Fyndes, Mr Megger-Bux and Dotty Fluster, the stewardess.

Page 123

The dead man's instructions are in the rolled-up newspaper. Sam realized this when she remembered this sentence in his message:
"There are further instructions rolled up in print."

Pages 124-125

To decipher the dead man's instructions, take the letters with dots beneath them and put them together, in order. This is what they say:

Vital information is hidden on this plane inside a yellow envelope. Find it and give it to your uncle. The final trivial answer is the key that will open the door.

Pages 126-127

From the newspaper message on pages 124-125, the twins know that the vital information is in a yellow envelope. This is hidden in the vulture's cage.

Pages 128-129

The answers to the trivial questions are shown below.

1	52	5	2	**Final answer**	
2	1	6	101		
3	420	7	8.25 (8¼)	1959	
4	2	8	5.75 (5¾)		

Pages 130-131

The answer to the riddle is the word LOCKER. The strange message tells Uncle Tom and the twins that they will find the proof they need in a (baggage) locker at the airport. The locker number is 13 (the same as the dead man's seat). The "key" to open the door of the locker is the number 1959 which is the final answer to the trivial landing game (see pages 128-129). The twins know this from the newspaper message on pages 124-125.

Pages 132-133

The thieves are Doctor Quickley, Pearl-Anne Plane and Ed Banger. The ancient treasure chart is in the Doctor's bag.

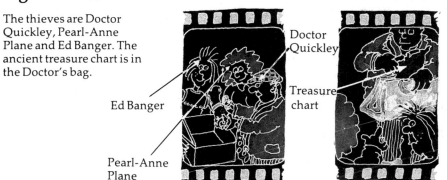

X marks the spot where the treasure is
buried. The black line shows the
course that Sam plotted to discover this.

Page 136

In his first message (see pages 116-117),
the dead man reveals his life is in danger
from the thieves. But only one of them
murdered him. Neither Pearl-Anne Plane

nor Ed Banger was at the drinks trolley
when the poison was added to the dead
man's drink, which means that Doctor
Quickley was the killer.

First published in 1986 by Usborne
Publishing Ltd, 20 Garrick Street, London
WC2E 9BJ, England.

Copyright 1986 Usborne Publishing Ltd.

The name Usborne and the device 🐝 are
Trade Marks of Usborne Publishing Ltd.

Printed in Belgium.